testify

do it again

First published in the United States in 2010 by Declaration Publishing
620 Camino De Los Mares Suite E #502
San Clemente, CA 92673
info@testifythebook.com
declarationpublishing.com
testifythebook.com

Library of Congress Control Number: 2010920312
ISBN: 978-0-615-34565-9
First Edition
Printed in China

Producer: Annie Kilroy
Editors and Writers: Anne Kilroy, Kalina Justice
Design, Layout and "Stones" Commentaries: Scott W. Bailey
Photography: Jeffrey Werve
Photo Director: Kalina Justice
Copy Editor: Dorine Imbach

Although the writers and publisher have made every effort to ensure the accuracy of the information contained in this book, we assume no responsibility for errors, inaccuracies, omissions, or any inconsistency herein. Further, we assume no liability for any loss, injury, or inconvenience sustained by the people who have testified in this book or any reader as a result of information or advice contained in Testify. Some of the names in this book have been changed to protect privacy.

testify

do it again

by Annie Kilroy
Declaration Publishing

Acknowledgments

Thank you!

My deepest appreciation to ...

Most importantly, my love to God, the author and finisher of our faith.

My friends who shared their testimonies.

Kalina Justice, my wonderful co-worker, who spent countless hours with me praying over each testimony as we wrote and edited. You are a treasure in whom I'm forever grateful.

Jeffrey Werve, for your brilliant photographs and tireless editing that captured every precious moment.

Scott Bailey, for your passion for the testimony and the creativity in which you masterfully brought all aspects of the project together for the book.

Pastor Roger Gales of Heritage Christian Fellowship; thank you for your encouragement. You are a faithful steward of God's miracles with a heart to see Him "do it again," down through the generations.

All the wonderful people from Heritage who gave of their time and talents: Tanya and Nancy, longtime friends and prayer partners, for their administrative skills; proofreaders Mary M., Cheryl, Mary D. and "the master eyes of San Clemente," Dorine; Jeff G. for mentoring me along the way; Dan G. for your wise legal counsel, Laura for translating and Troy for Scripture research. Thanks to Nina and Amy for being there, and finally models Emily and Sierra. We could not have completed this project without your help and countless others. You are all shining stars!

Gia Lucy, who opened up a whole new world of books beyond just reading.

Pastor Bill Johnson and Bethel Church, Redding, for your heart, example and teachings on the testimonies of God's miracles. The spiritual atmosphere of Bethel feels like a glimpse of heaven here on earth.

My wonderful children and grandchildren, who have brought love and joy to my life.

Dedication

They overcame him by the blood of the lamb
and by the word of their testimony;
Revelation 12:11a NIV

Table of Contents

TOC continued

Introduction

Testify

Like many of us I love a good people story. To read of triumph and victory over life circumstances warms my heart. The difference for me between a newsworthy story and a testimony is the power and revelation of the nature of God. What He has declared in His Word from the beginning is eternal and prophetic as it is passed down from generation to generation. The testimony creates an excitement and expectancy to see God "do it again." It has everlasting life, and when you become a Christian you are related to the God who makes signs and miracles happen. Talk about a heritage!

The people represented in TESTIFY, are just ordinary people like you and me who have faced the same life challenges we hear about every day. What makes their stories different is that they serve an extraordinary God. They stand victoriously and give their personal testimonies of faith so that we all might be encouraged.

Definition

Testify

The New American Webster Dictionary

Testify – to give testimony under oath, attest to the facts, and give evidence of.

Testimony – 1. A statement under oath by a witness.

2. Evidence; proof.

3. Open declaration, as of faith.

The Hebrew root word for "testimony" **הנע** transliterated **`anah (aw-naw')**, means to answer, respond, speak, shout or "do it again."

Memorial Stones

Testify

"Go over before the ark of the LORD your God into the middle of the Jordan. Each of you is to take up a stone on his shoulder, according to the number of the tribes of the Israelites, to serve as a sign among you. In the future, when your children ask you, 'What do these stones mean?' tell them that the flow of the Jordan was cut off before the ark of the covenant of the LORD. When it crossed the Jordan, the waters of the Jordan were cut off. These stones are to be a memorial to the people of Israel forever."

Joshua 4:5-7 NIV

It began hundreds of years before when God had prophesied to Abraham about delivering the children of Israel to a future promised land. For over 400 years they had been in bondage to Egypt's tyranny and oppression. God had brought the promised deliverer in Moses, but now it was his protégé, Joshua, much younger and less experienced, who was to lead the people across the final obstacle into the land. The Jordan river raging with overflow of the monsoon season stood between them and their promise. God had given Joshua the power to accomplish the task at hand; he needed to believe it and walk in it. As Joshua obeyed, miraculously the Jordan river stopped as if an invisible dam was present, and the people walked across on dry ground. The promise was true. Look what the Lord had done.

After they crossed there was another task the LORD instructed Joshua to do, "When you cross the river have twelve men each grab a stone from the center of the river and stack them on the opposite side as a sign and remembrance of what God did today." Memorial stones. They are to be a testimony passed down from generation to generation, of God's goodness and faithfulness.

When someone through the ages would encounter these memorial stones the question would be raised, "What happened here?" And each generation would pass down the stories of the God of promise. God wanted His people to not only remember Him, but to know Him.

This very same God is still fulfilling promises today. This is your God too! He is searchable and findable. He knows you and you can know Him.

TESTIFY the book has 22 testimonies written from 29 hearts telling of God's greatness and faithfulness. Each one of these people has been called, like you, to share their God story. God is active with us; every one of us has a testimony, a monument, a pile of stones. This book is a memorial stone to the Father in heaven who adores you and calls you.

Chosen for Your Glory

Jer and Kat

Jer

It all began back in 1968 when I thought it would be a good idea to get hit by a car, break my hip and femur so I could end up in the hospital and meet this cute nurse's aide named Kathy Kirwan. I fell in love during those twenty-one days in the hospital. We got married and started a family. Our first-born was Steve and eight years later came Joshua. I wish that I could tell you that our marriage was perfect, but I can't. We had our struggles and even a six-month break-up. Things were not going well and we knew we needed more. One day in February 1981, Kat and I decided to attend a little church in San Clemente, California. It was there that we both accepted Christ as our Savior.

Things got better as we attended church regularly and I cut way back on my drinking and cocaine use. For me it was a process that would take many years until I really got it and completely surrendered my life to God. I made a decision to stop living life selfishly and allow God to heal our family. From this point on we have never taken our relationship for granted. We realized how blessed we were to have and love each other. This love gave us strength and helped us to endure through many seasons of life together. However…nothing could have prepared us for the diagnosis of stage four throat cancer.

Kat

When Jer told me that the biopsy was positive for cancer, I felt like time stood still! This was my love, my husband, and the man I have always affectionately called "my boyfriend." He had never been sick a day in his life. We both held each other and wept. That's when we cried out to the One who is in control and asked for supernatural wisdom. At that time I wrote on our family message board several things that God had put on my heart:

Love and serve each other!

Keep our eyes fixed on Jesus – do not waver!

Jer is indestructible until God is done with him – no fear!

Committed to trust God no matter what!

May the God of hope fill you with all joy and peace as you trust in him,
so that you may overflow with hope by the power of the Holy Spirit.
Romans 15:13 NIV

We visually focused on these truths until it was all over.

Then began our cancer fast track. We walked through four surgeries, including a tonsillectomy, a porta-cath to deliver the chemo, a feeding tube in Jer's abdomen and removal of the suspect lymph node in his neck. The doctor told him that cancer never starts in the lymph nodes. It always begins somewhere else. Right after Christmas we began a heavy schedule of intense radiation. The radiation required us to go in five times a week over a period of seven weeks and that included chemotherapy.

I watched my husband boyfriend ... best friend quietly suffer *so very bravely*

The battle between fear and faith would overwhelm me at times. That's when my dearest friends and the body of Christ would hold my arms up, and those moments of fear would be replaced with the faith to carry on. I watched my husband, boyfriend, best friend quietly suffer so very bravely. I told Jer that Jesus and he were my heroes!

Jer

I received prayer from all over the world, thanks to the internet and good friends who put out the word. I learned to seek God's presence continually as my faith turned to total trust in Him and His Word and He became my constant companion. One night a group of men came over to our house to pray for my upcoming PET scan, which would show if there were any cancer cells in my body. This is how that went.

My friend Jeff called me and asked if some men could meet at our house and pray for me regarding the scan I would have the following Monday. Jeff and I had been talking at church about his victory over cancer. He recently was declared cancer free! As a result of Jeff's miracle he had formed a men's prayer group that go out and pray for people. I was honored to be on that list.

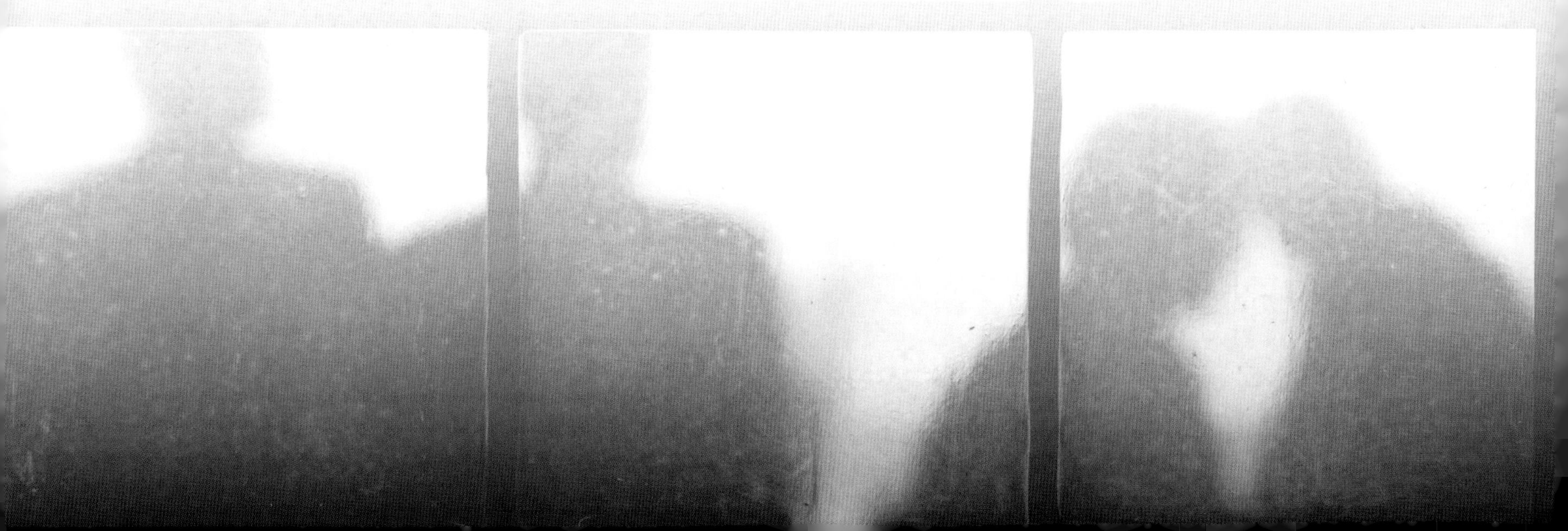

One by one, the men filled our living room. There were seven men and Gavin, Jeff's young son. We had a sweet time of fellowship before I shared exactly what was going on with me and about the upcoming scan. It was a very comfortable time since I considered each man there a friend.

I sat in our comfy little Hawaiian rocker and they gathered around me, laid hands on me, anointed me with oil and began to pray. There were many requests made unto the Lord. The Holy Spirit was asked to show up, and He did not disappoint. Someone in the group prayed that the Lord would give me dreams and visions about the scan. I really don't feel like I am a person that has spiritual-type dreams or visions, but once, in fact, years ago I had a vision that turned out to be very practical. It was regarding a stoppage in our sewer pipe. The Lord showed me in a dream the exact location and what the stoppage was. The next day I was able to cut open the pipe and pulled out a four-foot tree root, patched it up and never had a sewer problem again!

Well, on the night the men came over to pray about my PET scan, I had a dream. It was definitely different. I do dream quite frequently; however, they usually are either nonsensical or just kind of crazy, like, where did that come from? In this dream, I was sitting in a seat outside a type of arena. It had a wooden floor and was about the size of a hockey rink. Sprinkled on the floor was a substance like a mixture of sand and sawdust, and people were seated around the arena. My seat was at one end and there was a man sitting next to me explaining what was going on. I never saw his face. Suddenly at the opposite end of the arena there appeared a machine, very similar to a Zamboni, except there was a small plow mounted on the front. There were flames about one foot high shooting up in front of the machine, and the driver would plow the sandy material and extinguish the flames as he worked his way to the end of the arena. The man seated next to me explained that this represented a cancer scan and if all the flames are extinguished when the machine reaches the end of the arena that person would be cancer free. This run was for someone else, but I didn't know who. The machine got to the end of the arena, where a goal might be, and all the flames were gone and there was an announcement over the PA system, CANCER FREE! And everyone applauded with joy. Now it was time for my scan and the machine started out again at the other end of the arena and was working its way toward the goal. Flames were being extinguished along the way and it was looking good. When it got to my end of the arena the machine was having trouble keeping the flames under control. Just before the machine got to the goal, the driver jumped off and grabbed what looked like a half sheet of plywood. He began to scrape the sandy material onto the flames. He was working really fast and finally the last flame was extinguished. Suddenly there was complete silence and the lights went out. I didn't know what to think, and then a very authoritative voice, not from the PA system, said very distinctly,

Suddenly there was complete silence and the lights went out.

I didn't know what to think, and then a very authoritative voice, not from the PA system, said very distinctly,

"There is no cancer in this man."

"There is no cancer in this man." I woke up and I knew God had answered that prayer. I couldn't wait to tell Kat, but it was 4:00 in the morning.

Later that week, my doctor called with the results of the scan. He said, "No cancer seen." It was just as God had spoken to me in my dream! CANCER FREE! Praise and honor and glory to the King!!

Kat and I were encouraged beyond any expectations that we may have had and truly felt so thankful for all the friends and church family that rallied beside us by bringing us meals, driving me to treatments, providing gas cards to help offset our expenses and most of all the many prayers that sustained us. We were blessed to become friends with a couple from our church, Donna and Dan. Donna went through the exact same treatment and supported us through our journey. I want to thank my wife, who is my girlfriend and best friend, for her unconditional love and support through this. I couldn't imagine going through this without her.

God spoke to me continually during this time. One Sunday morning at church I asked Him, "Why did my friend Jeff and I have to go through cancer? His answer was very clear. "Because I chose you for My Glory." (John 9:1-3) I'm thankful I have been able to return to work. My girlfriend, Kat, and I enjoy riding our tandem bike, and I'm back surfing again. I recently received a second scan that came back clear. God has been incredibly faithful through it all, and as C.H. Spurgeon said, "I can thank my God for every storm that has wrecked me upon the Rock, Christ Jesus!"

"Thanks for praying for me,
Girlfriend"
"I love you, Boyfriend"

created to worship

Carlos

The lure to associate with gang members and a desire to fit in was often overwhelming. This lifestyle for a young Latino male is very strong, providing security and family. This is really all he ever wanted…to fit in. Carlos became an angry teenager, and if he didn't turn his life around, was on his way to trouble.

Carlos is a twenty-three-year-old Christian recording artist. He recently appeared on ALMAVISION, a Mexican Christian television station worshiping Jesus Christ with his music. As a new songwriter Carlos has a positive message of salvation and hope to share with his audience. He believes he was created to worship and he knows personally the One who gives him the songs to write. Five years ago, he didn't have a voice, didn't sing, and certainly didn't go to church.

Carlos was born in the town of Iguala, Mexico. His parents immigrated to the United States when he was just two years old, settling in Southern California in the city of Dana Point. The transition was hard for the family and eventually the parents split up. Carlos lived with his mother, who imparted good values and raised him with a Catholic background. He didn't want to do anything that would break his mother's heart, yet the streets outside had such a pull.

it began in junior high WHEN HE WAS FIRST INTRODUCED to the GANG LIFESTYLE

The lure to associate with gang members and a desire to fit in was often overwhelming. This lifestyle for a young Latino male is very strong, providing security and family. This is really all he ever wanted…to fit in. Carlos became an angry teenager, and if he didn't turn his life around, was on his way to trouble.

It began in junior high, when he was first introduced to the gang lifestyle. Kids were selling drugs on campus and doing them in the bathroom. Alcohol was consumed in water bottles. In high school it was cocaine. Many of the gang members were violent and liked to fight. At this time he was drifting, without goals or ambition. Turning seventeen, Carlos reached his lowest point, when his mother was diagnosed with cancer. She had been his rock, and now she was sick.

How could God allow this to happen to her? He felt helpless, blaming God for everything, especially for his mom's battle with cancer. Being a proud and strong young man, Carlos thought somehow he could make her better…but it didn't work out that way.

This was a dark and frustrating time for him. He chose to hang out with people who would blaspheme God and ridicule the Bible. They all listened to satanic music and this seemed to fuel his hostility. He desperately wanted friends and family, yet he was so angry with everyone. Weekend parties and fighting were a way of life. He needed a dad to provide parenting, but it seemed too late for that. Anyway, he had no relationship with his father. Carlos was desperate and headed for trouble. If something didn't happen soon, he would get caught and end up in jail.

One day his dad came knocking on the front door and told him he had become a Christian. Carlos felt very hostile toward his dad and really didn't want to be around him, but for some reason that day, when his dad asked him to go to church, he went. Maybe it was the lunch invitation afterward. Dressed in gang-banger clothes and a beanie, he sat in the back of the church, listening to the message of salvation, that Jesus had died on the cross for him. How could that be? For me? Why would Christ die for me? There must be a logical answer.

During the next few weeks, as Carlos spent more time with his dad, he noticed a big change. His father used to be so distant, angry, and showed little compassion for him. These last few weeks Carlos realized his dad demonstrated love, peace and joy. His father was a different man. It was easier being with him and so father and son continued going to church on Sundays in the hopes that their relationship would get better.

One Sunday, Carlos entered the church building hoping to find that same peace he had seen in his father. The pastor shared a message that day on how Jesus was the only one who could fill the void in our hearts and give us a reason to live, that we were created to worship HIM. Carlos felt so broken and desperately wanted to be whole.

He began to understand what the pastor was talking about, how he needed to surrender his life to Christ. As those very words were spoken, he broke down and wept, tears streaming down his face. Later he would say that he had not cried since he was 10 years old. Now his anger and pride were being washed off, and at that moment Carlos invited Jesus Christ as his Lord and Savior into his life. That is where the Lord did the first miracle in him.

That day, after Carlos dedicated His life to the Lord, he couldn't wait to go home and share his experience with his mom. She also received Jesus into her life, and for a year they were able to go to church together until she passed away from cancer.

During that time much reconciliation took place within his family. Carlos rejoices knowing his mom is resting in heaven with her Lord, and that brings him comfort. God has mended his relationship with his father and now they enjoy spending time together. Recently, the Lord has blessed Carlos with a wonderful wife. He is a contented man, no longer filled with anger, but walking in the peace of God.

As Carlos was learning so much about the Christian life and desiring to know his spiritual gifts, others would comment on his voice as he sang during worship, telling him that he had a beautiful voice. He was surprised and encouraged to hear that. He knew he felt good when he was singing to God, but was that really his voice? It sounded pretty good! With encouragement he began to explore voice lessons. He was lost in worshiping his heavenly Father and knew in his heart that his purpose was being fulfilled.

As this relationship grew deeper, God began to gift songs to him, not just downloading the lyrics but the music as well. Carlos knew this was a miracle from God because he could feel the power flowing through him, as songs would be written sometimes within five to ten minutes. It was the divine creativity of God, because he knew couldn't do it on his own.

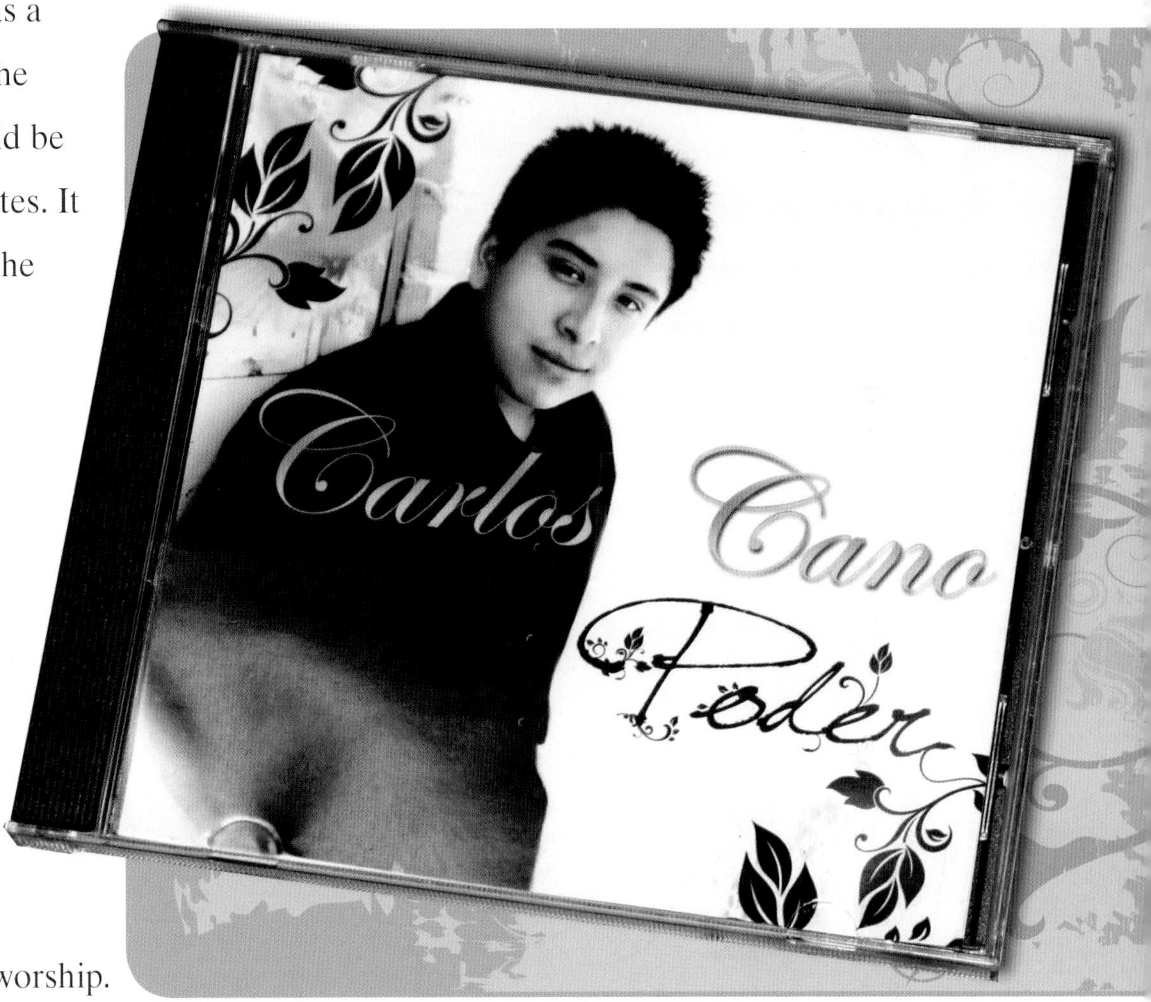

Shortly thereafter, the pastor of his church put him in touch with a recording producer. They began working together and within three months Carlos recorded his first album, PODER (power). He now travels to other churches sharing his love of God, giving Him all the glory, honor and praise. Carlos would be the first to say that, without HIM, he might not be here today…for he was created to worship.

I will praise you, O Lord, among the nations; I will sing of you among the peoples.
For great is your love, reaching to the heavens; your faithfulness reaches to the skies.
Be exalted, O God, above the heavens; let glory be over all the earth.

Psalm 57: 9-11 NIV

A Woman With A Secret

Minka

My name is Minka. I want to tell you about a secret that I have held in my heart for seventy-eight years. I pray it will encourage you to never lose hope. God our Father is a faithful, loving and merciful God, who watches over His word to perform it. For we live in His kingdom and under His sovereign rule.

God works in mysterious ways, His wonders to perform. Who can fathom the depth of His wisdom or His love as He works all things out according to His purpose and our good? I was given the opportunity to review my life of ninety-seven years because of something that happened a long time ago. Can we know the destiny of lives, families, cities and nations? The Bible states that the prayers of a righteous man avail much. It also says, "Seek ye first the kingdom of God and His righteousness and all others things shall be added unto you." I pondered those words and kept them in my heart. My life took a dramatic turn in July 2006.

I was born of pure Dutch ancestors, who were born and raised in Holland. My father immigrated to America, followed by my mother, who was pregnant with me and an older brother. My father worked on a dairy farm. When I was 1½ years old, my sister was born. She was nine days old when my father drowned in a lake. With three babies, my mother, who had not yet mastered English, went to work for an elderly German farmer. Though she did not speak English, she spoke German as well as her native Dutch.

As children, we knew what it was to work—before and after school, from sun up to sun down. We hauled water, wood, and coal because those were the days of no running water, electricity, or gas in the homes. We picked potatoes, shucked wheat, corn and whatever else was planted that year.

I was traumatized **bewildered** and ***scared***

When I was fourteen, the man my mother worked for retired and she married another Dutchman. Together they started a dairy farm. Not only did he gain a wife, but three well trained farmhands as well, who were good at milking cows.

When we graduated from eighth grade at our country schoolhouse, we were told that high school was for city kids who had nothing else to do. Attending high school was out of the question for us; we had too much work to do.

At sixteen years old, my mother sent me to a sewing class a woman was teaching. I do not recollect the reason, but one day the sewing class hosted a picnic by the lake. While there, another girl and I went for a walk to the skating rink. Later, as we were heading back to the group, walking amongst the trees, we were raped by two men. We had never seen them before, didn't know them, nor ever saw them again.

I was traumatized, bewildered, and scared. I could never mention this to my mother because we never talked about such things. I had never even seen a pregnant woman. Long dresses and aprons covered pregnancy. Women continued to work hard in those days without any of our modern "push-button" appliances.

I do not remember all the details surrounding my pregnancy. My mother went to our German Lutheran pastor and together they determined the course I was to take. I was checked into a Lutheran Home and an Adoptive Agency for girls. I had never been away from home or my mother, but I was at the mercy of their decision.

I grew up overnight. Where was I going? What did life hold for me?

Fortunately, the Lutheran Home was filled with love, prayers, and kindness—the kind of love you could see, feel and touch. The lady in charge talked with me, explained certain things, and reasoned with me. She lovingly explained the advantages of giving my child up for adoption. I made a very painful decision.

When my baby daughter was one month old, I gave her a name. She then was given to a Norwegian Lutheran pastor and his wife for adoption.

I went on with my life, keeping in touch with the agency to track my daughter's growth and welfare. They acknowledged every letter—some with news if there was any, and some without. My daughter never left my heart or life. Every year on her birthday I wondered where and how she was.

On May 22, 2006, I woke up and asked the Lord if He would let me see her. If He allowed me to see her, I made a solemn promise I would never bother her or her family. Then I dismissed the thought and went about the affairs of the day. Then, on July 2nd, my phone rang and a message was left on my recorder. It was a woman saying she was trying to locate me.

A while later the phone rang again. The man on the line asked me, "Are you Minka?"

I said, "Speaking."

It was my daughter's son! He had spent six months trying to get records released through the courts in order to find me. After a few questions on both sides, he put his mother on the phone. This was my very own daughter. It was a nostalgic moment to hear her voice, even though she was a grown seventy-seven-year-old woman. Her adoptive parents had given her a new name. I learned that the adoptive parents were a couple who had two sons and desperately wanted a little girl. Her father was a godly, prayerful man known as Peter, "the Rock." He was a man of prayer, a pastor and an evangelist.

My daughter told me she had six children, all who are successful, highly educated and married with children. I was proud to learn that some of my grandchildren have achieved successes in education. One was a coach, one a teacher and some professors. All these were accomplishments for which I was not afforded the opportunity.

Three of my grandsons made careers for themselves in the military. One is a Colonel, a graduate from West Point. Another works for Boeing and NASA, in charge of building the International Space Station. He was in charge of one of the pieces of hardware that was installed on the station in 2007. The hardware provided structure for the station as well as generated power to keep the astronauts alive. And as only God would have it, one of my grandsons is an astronaut. He manned four flights into space, with a total of thirteen million miles, going around the world 517 times.

When I got older and left the farm, I married and had two more children. I have a son and a daughter who also married and blessed me with grandchildren. My husband was a fighter pilot in WWII and a drafting engineer. After a long battle with illness my husband finally succumbed to cancer. My wonderful son passed away in 2000. Through all of this I found comfort in the Lord. My life was a challenge, hampered by lack of education. In spite of this, I was placed in various managerial positions. I worked for over eighteen years in a school district and retired at the age of sixty-six.

Years later, I found myself with a little granddaughter to raise and educate. So I returned to work at a local Kmart. I worked as a cashier for another thirteen years and retired again at eighty-seven.

As I look back, I see God's guidance and direction leading me to a higher spiritual realm, a higher spiritual maturity, for such a time as this. This was the moment my entire family would be reunited.

After tracking me down, my precious grandson, the Colonel, and his family brought my beautiful daughter to see me. What a precious time we had. I felt she had just come home for a visit because she had never really left my heart. Here was the moment when my two daughters would meet.

Does the Lord watch over us? Does the Lord answer prayer? Indeed He does. I have been blessed by a wonderful family, friends and in life. I have a feeling there are more chapters to be added to this story. May God richly bless everyone who is without hope. God always makes a way when you think there isn't one.

Imagine what would have happened if this rape had occurred to me today.

Imagine what would have happened if this rape had occurred to me today. I probably would have been advised to have an abortion. My daughter would not have been born and the world would not have known the wonderful and productive family that resulted from her birth, a family the world can be proud of. I became the proud grandmother of 18 great grandchildren and 12 grandchildren. I am blessed beyond measure. To God be the glory. Blessings to all others who had a part of my life in Him, held in His hands and grafted into His plan.

After my daughter and all the others left, I was alone when the Lord said to me, "Now you can forgive him." And, I did. I hoped he too had found the Lord and was serving Him.

I wondered, since then, had he watched the space shuttle go up with the astronauts not knowing that one of them was his grandson?

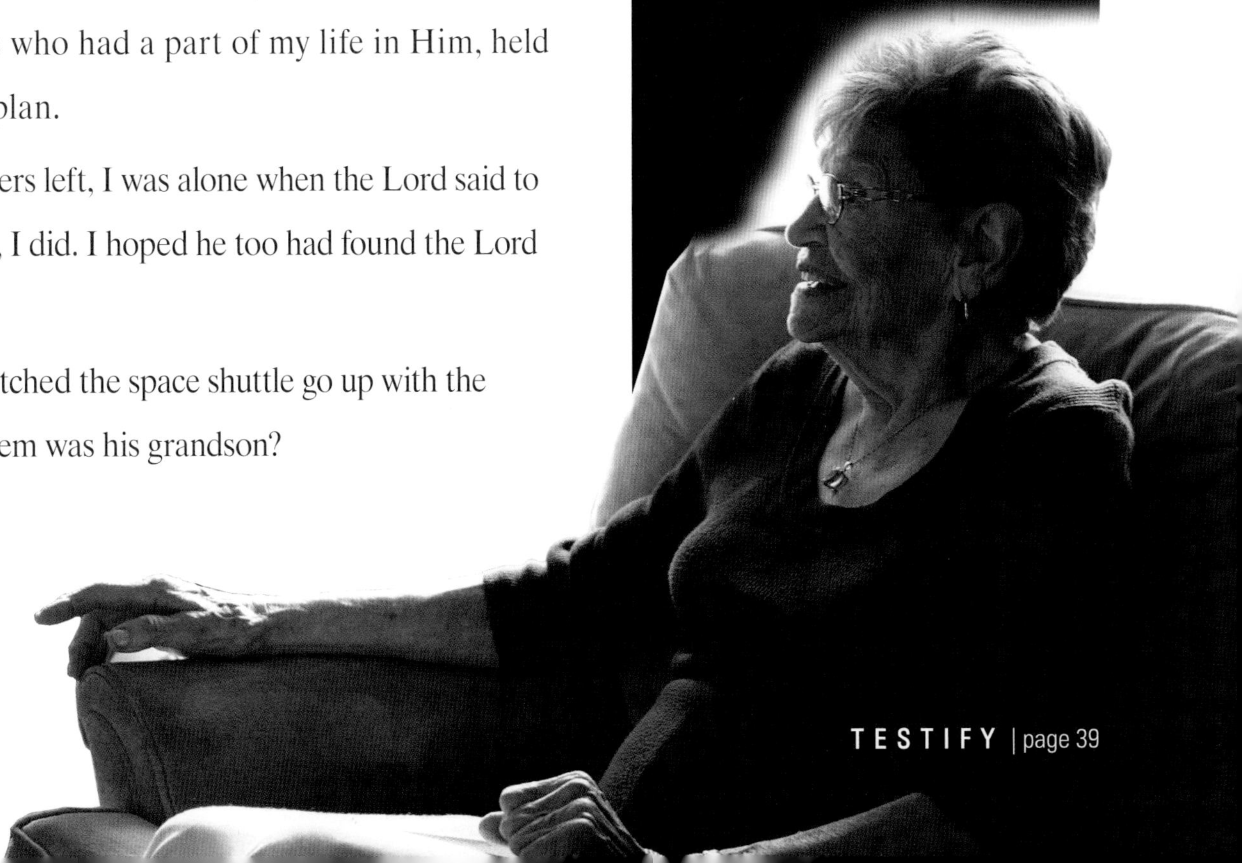

Hope!

I leave you with these words of hope. Hope is the ingredient that gets us up in the morning. When we know that God cares, but we haven't seen any evidence of it in the last few days, weeks, sometimes months or years, hope drives us onward when we want to stop and quit. Hope keeps our dreams alive while we are waiting. We need hope because we can't always control the timetable.

As for God His way is perfect, the word of the LORD is flawless,
He is our shield for all who take refuge in him.
2 Samuel 22:31 NIV

May these words give someone hope and a new lease on life. For our Lord and Savior promised to never leave or forsake us, and sent the Holy Spirit to guide and direct us. The Father's love, mercy, and grace endure unto all generations. And He is still in control of all things now and forever.

May your prayer be: "Father, open my eyes and my heart to see who you are. For we lay our cares at your feet and the finished work at Calvary."

May my testimony give someone hope today. God sees your heart and hears your prayers. Seek Him, praise Him, and honor Him. Never doubt, for He has a plan and a purpose for your life and is working out your destiny day after day, one step at a time.

God Bless you all.

... had he watched the space shuttle go up with the astronauts not knowing that one of them was his grandson?

A Precious Jewel

Kendra

I am 24 years old and grew up in the Church. A few weeks ago I was at a friend's Bible study and there were several German exchange students there as guests. During the study we began to discuss the topic of pro life vs. pro choice. I was so excited and began to express my feelings on the subject. A girl that was visiting asked me, "Where is it written in the Bible that we are not to have abortions?" I explained to her that the Bible does not speak on abortions but rather there are scriptures that declare how God values human life. I began by sharing these scriptures:

For you created my inmost being; you knit me together in my mother's womb. I praise you because I am fearfully and wonderfully made; your works are wonderful, I know that full well. My frame was not hidden from you when I was made in the secret place. When I was woven together in the depths of the earth, your eyes saw my unformed body. All the days ordained for me were written in your book before one of them came to be. How precious to me are your thoughts, O God! How vast is the sum of them! Were I to count them, they would outnumber the grains of sand. When I awake, I am still with you.

Psalm 139:13-18 NIV

Before I formed you in the womb I knew you, before you were born I set you apart;
I appointed you as a prophet to the nations.
Jeremiah 1:5 NIV

To me these verses are very vital in my life. They express a deep, personal, and intimate relationship that we have with the Lord before we are born. He knows every detail about us. He created us in His image for His delight and His glory. Each one of us He designed intricately and uniquely. We are His creation.

I was asked by the leader of the study to go a little deeper and share the reality behind my opinion.

Here is a portion of my journal that I shared...

October 2nd, 2007

I haven't started my period yet and it's been almost 2 months. Only You know what that means. I'm scared though. I'm ready to accept my part from You, Lord, whether that means I'm pregnant or my body is doing something really weird. I'm scared and ashamed. I didn't have to sleep with him. I knew what I was doing. I'm sad that I hurt myself; I don't even know what I would do if I were pregnant. Should I keep it? Should I give it up? What if it's a boy, or a girl? Only You know the truth. Should I tell everyone and suffer the disgrace?

All of a sudden
I realized what
was happening.
I was giving her this
present, a jewel –
a precious jewel

Exactly one month after this journal entry I found out I was pregnant. I took a pregnancy test and it turned blue right away. My then boyfriend and I had sex only one time. That just goes to show you, it does happen! My daughter's name is Cadence Grace. After a lot of prayer, guidance and counsel we realized that our relationship was not adequate to raise her. It wasn't just our relationship, our maturity; we wanted more for her and so we placed her up for adoption. We felt she would need more from us than what we were able to provide. Looking for the best possible parents, we interviewed two couples, sent them questions, and got to know them. Finally, we decided on one. They were a Christian family who could not have children. They were kind, loving, and really respectful of our decision.

THERE IS NOTHING YOU CAN DO to make GOD LOVE YOU MORE LOVE YOU LESS

One day over lunch with the adoptive mom, she shared with me that she was getting more sleep now in preparation for the baby to come home. Wow! It hit me so hard. She was going to be a mom! All of a sudden I realized what was happening. I was giving her this present, a jewel — a precious jewel that had been knit together in my womb. For me to see the delight in her eyes, to witness how much she and her husband love Cadence, I can honestly say that there is no way that this could have happened without the Lord.

Today Cadence Grace is over a year old, and I stand here before you to let you know, this is my life. It's messy and it's real. I sinned and screwed up. I paid for it big-time. I got pregnant and placed my daughter up for adoption. Sometimes life is really, really hard, so hard it makes my heart ache. And other times, I'm so full of joy I feel like singing and dancing because I love life. The Lord is The Redeemer. He has redeemed me. He has blessed my life. I meditate upon the words of Phillip Yancey in his book *What's So Amazing About Grace?* "There is nothing you can do to make God love you more, and there is nothing that you can do to make God love you less."

These are words I know to be true.

Standing Stone

Testify

Always be prepared to give an answer to everyone who asks you to give the reason for the hope that you have. But do this with gentleness and respect,
1 Peter 3:15b NIV

A witness, in the sense that I am using the word, is a man whose life and faith are so completely one that when the challenge comes to step out and testify for his faith, he does so, disregarding all risks, accepting all consequences. —*Whittaker Chambers*

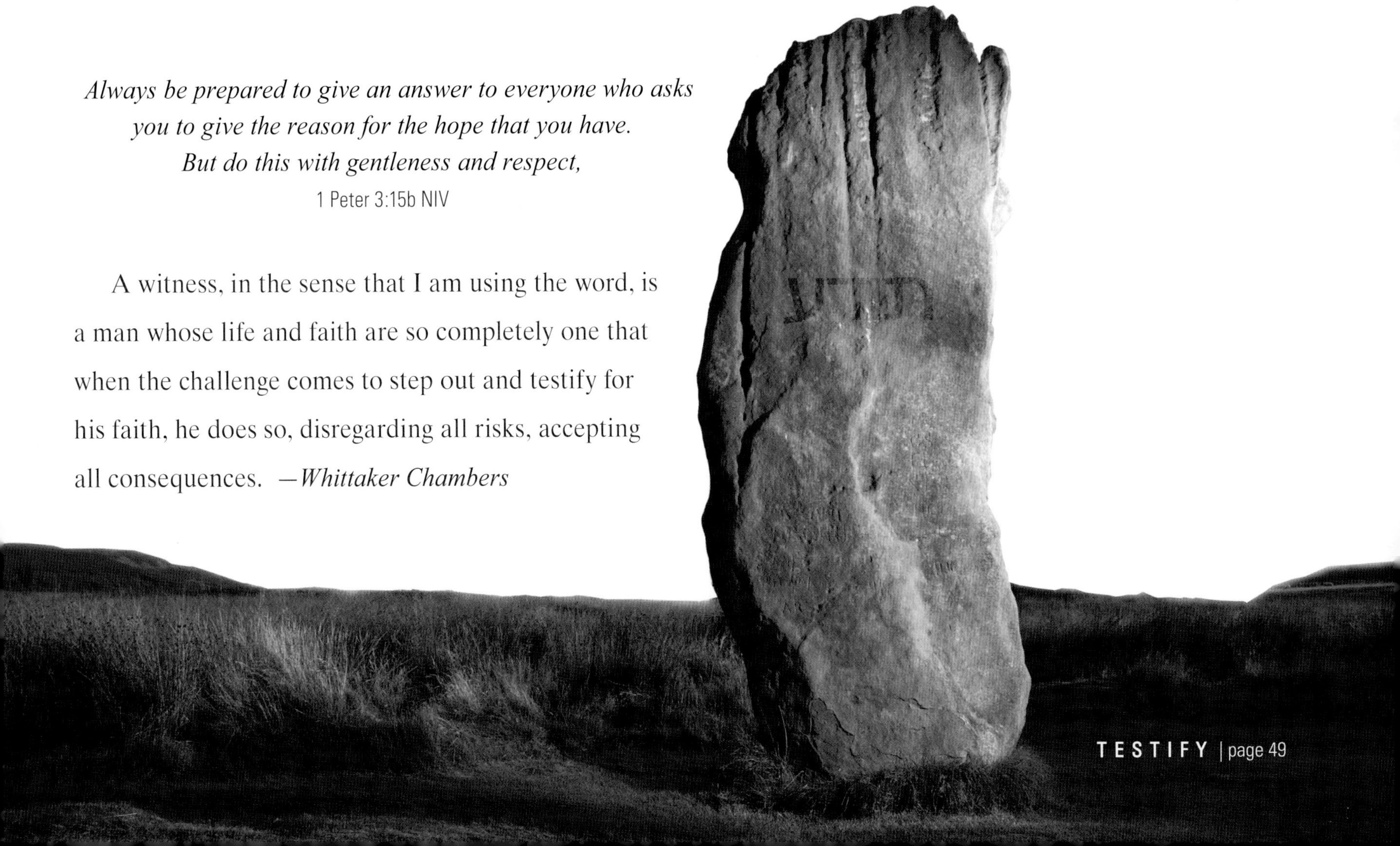

No Excuses

Tom and Allison

This is our story. We offer no excuses, simply an explanation of our journey.

Tom

I was raised in Capistrano Beach, one of nine perfect angels. Our house was never quiet. Sibling rivalry was alive and well. When I was six years old my father left for Vietnam. We wouldn't speak again until I was twenty-five. My mother did the best she could. She raised us with a Catholic upbringing, an iron fist and not much room for diplomacy or understanding. I was an angry child and my brothers nicknamed me Bulldog.

Allison

I grew up in Laguna Niguel. I was the youngest of four children. Both my parents were alcoholics and they were not "happy drunks." Our home was filled with chaos and confusion, yelling, and things being thrown. I remember when my step-dad was in one of his rages and ripped off some cupboard doors, only to put them back up by morning as if nothing ever happened, and no one said a word. I learned to be quiet, not make any trouble, and oftentimes look the other way.

TOM

We met in 1984. Two years later, we were married. This was a scary time for me. Not only was I to take care of Allison, but she was pregnant with our son. Fundamentally, everything seemed right. We loved God, went to church, and loved our family. Yet, we brought into our marriage our personal baggage and the leftovers from our childhood. Not wanting to make the same mistakes, we were determined to make it work. Over the next twenty years, we would be tested in these areas.

ALLISON

Life was pretty good. I loved being a wife and a mother. I went back to work when our youngest was four. It was there I found a false identity in the people I worked with. I wanted to be at work more than I wanted to be home. Tom and I were already distant and this created a bigger wedge. I felt lonely and empty in my marriage and we had no communication skills and no intimacy. I couldn't go to Tom with my feelings. I went the lowest I could go, and eleven years ago I had an affair. I was very emotionally attached to the man in my affair. I didn't like Tom very much. At the same time, I wanted to know what God desired from me. He very clearly told me to stay in my marriage. So, I was obedient and I stayed. I confessed everything to Tom.

TOM

I was crushed, devastated, angry and heartbroken. This is the first time in my life I would share my deep feelings. I chose to stay with Allison for our kids, not knowing at the time I was scared to be alone. This meant that I didn't have to deal with my abandonment and rejection issues from the past. We threw ourselves into church and did the things our counselor told us to do. There was some healing in our marriage; life went on and the pain slowly went away.

ALLISON

We started going to Heritage Christian Fellowship five years ago. I couldn't escape my loneliness, guilt, and shame. I was encouraged to see Pastor Phil for counseling and went to the Monday night recovery group. I didn't know where God would take me over the next three years. God began to

remove layers off of me and I began to rediscover myself. I went deeper with God and He showed me who I was in Him. I was becoming whole, finally growing up and being set free. The healthier I got, the further away Tom went.

TOM

I became very distant from Allison. I was not interested in spending any time with her and was not being a good husband. I was a walking zombie. I couldn't live with myself any longer. I confessed to Allison that I now was having an affair. The truth was finally out and the weight of despair was lifted, not knowing what choices Allison would make for herself.

ALLISON

I knew God had prepared me for this very moment. I chose to stay. God had given me beautiful relationships, people who held me up when I just couldn't stand on my own. He gave me faith and a promise: "You two will be amazing, if you stay the course." I knew God could change this man. He had already done a work in me. I knew He could save this marriage. And even if Tom chose not to do the work, I would still be okay.

TOM

I chose to stay in the marriage. We had tools and a plan, but it was a slow transition. I had an internal battle going on. The enemy did not want to let me go. As I surrendered to God, He began to change me. I began to walk in God's truth and not out of emotions and feelings. Part of this process included getting real with our kids, nineteen and twenty-one at the time. We told them about both of our affairs. This was an extremely difficult time for our family. Today we still see the pain in them, neither one wanting to discuss it. We remain consistent in our walk and our commitment to one another, with the hope that one day, they too will be healed.

ALLISON

Tom and I shared this with our children, not only to uncover the lies but to break the chains of generational sin. I could not have withstood any of this without Christ and the people He put in my life. If I have learned anything, it's about relationship — with Him and with others. We don't have to do it alone. God has not only restored our marriage, He's given us things we've never had before. By His love, grace and strength, my husband and I are together today.

TOM

You may be asking yourself, how could both of them have had an affair? It is because we never faced the deeply-rooted issues of our childhood: abandonment, anger, rejection, lack of nurturing, etc. We didn't have the proper tools to heal and be whole.

Since then, we believe in and have seen miracles. Our marriage is a living testimony to all who may struggle with the same issues we had. To God be the glory! We firmly believe God wants us to do the work. It needs to be impartation, not imitation. It needs to stick. We will continue to pursue the precious gift of true intimacy with our Heavenly Father and with each other. The peace and freedom we experience is difficult to explain but easy to obtain if you are willing to face life's challenges and get real.

Counseling: At times we didn't like what we heard, but we needed to remain humble.

Separation: We were so enmeshed, we needed to come apart, take responsibility for ourselves and then come back together.

Journaling: What is it? It is the expression of feelings on paper. Then, it is listening to God speak. Later, you can reflect and see how far you've come and see how God worked.

Prayer: Pray! Pray! Pray! Prayer gives you intimacy with God.

Accountability: Have one or two people to get real with. Remember, confidentiality is the key.

Recovery Group: There you receive tools to deal with deeply-rooted issues and strongholds.

Crossroads

Beatrice

Beatrice was angry with God. How could He let this happen to her and her family? They struggled so hard. Her husband worked all the time and they lived "by his hard work and sweat from his forehead." It has been that way ever since they came to the United States. Over a year ago, the doctors diagnosed her autistic son with epilepsy as well as asthma. It seemed like one chronic illness piled on top of another. Feeling hopeless she became overwhelmed with thinking there was no way out. She was lost and drifting away from God.

The day the doctor told me about my son's condition I believed in my head and my heart that my son was dead! The news was devastating. I screamed out at the top of my lungs hoping to drown out what I had just heard. I cried and cried wanting it not to be true and pleading that it would all go away. The doctor and nurse helped calm me down and after a while sent me home with my son.

On the way back to my house, I had to walk across railroad tracks, and seeing the tracks gave me an idea. How easily I could end all of this pain by throwing myself and my son in front of the train.

I made up my mind ...
... to throw myself
in front of the train
and take my son with me

This could be a way out. I thought no one should have to live like a slave to these diseases. And what about my life? I was a prisoner with no key to open my cell door. I began thinking about all the suffering that my husband and daughter would have to bear. My husband already works very hard at two jobs just to make ends meet. I made up my mind that it was okay to throw myself in front of the train and take my son with me.

Then, something very strange happened to me at that very moment, just when I was so determined to execute my plan. An amazing presence, very heavy, like a super-heavy coat covered my body. The weight of it was so heavy that I had to sit down or I would fall. I let myself fall onto a rock that was nearby. When I was seated, I heard an audible voice. Or, maybe it was a thought that had a sound. I wasn't sure because there was no one around. The voice said, "What if your son survives and doesn't die here at the railroad tracks? Who would take care of him then?"

I cried and cried, holding my son in my arms. I was at a crossroads. There was a battle going on in my mind. While I was saddened by these questions, the reality of that moment was life-changing. I believe that it was the voice of God speaking to me. If so, then where did that other terrifying thought come from?

I prayed and cried out to God and told Him that I could not bear the responsibility of taking care of my son by myself. Instantly He heard my prayer and answered me.

Call to me and I will answer you and tell you great and unsearchable things you do not know.
Jeremiah 33:3 NIV

I was filled with comfort and hope, and after a while I was able to get up and take my son home. I had a supernatural experience that day and it changed my life forever. For the first time in my life, I felt the presence of God standing with me that day on the railroad tracks. He delivered us from evil because of His love and compassion. He will never abandon me. His Word says that He will not give us more that we can handle. That is why I returned to Him. I have faith for the things I cannot see or understand. I realize that God never leaves us, even in the most terrible moments. In fact, that is when He is right there next to us, holding us up, getting us through. What God wants is for us to tell Him, "Here I am; take my problems." I'm so thankful for how He intervened in my life that day when I was overwhelmed with hopelessness and bad thoughts.

Last fall I had no money and I knew that Christmas was coming and my children would have no gifts. I prayed to God and, once again,

HE ANSWERED my prayers.

Today, we still have all the doctors' appointments, blood tests, medications, and they are tiresome. My son is on so many medications. The difference now is that I have surrendered to God and am at peace. There are wonderful people that God has used as instruments in our lives. People are praying for us and showing us unconditional love.

I belong to a group called Fiesta Familiar where mothers with children who have disabilities gather together to support one another. My son does not recognize his diagnosis or his illness. In his first early years, when I discovered my son had autism, I lived in frustration. I could not comprehend the disease and didn't understand why I wasn't able to communicate with him. I had to repeat myself so many times. Now, because of prayers and his medication, I understand him better and I have more patience with him.

I would like to use my story to help other parents of children with autism, especially those who have just found out the shocking news. "Believe and expect of God; only He can help us." We don't know why these children suffer and we can't believe that God would allow them to suffer either.

We need faith. I attend my support group every Saturday and go to church once a week. These relationships help to encourage me, and my faith is so much greater than just these acts.

We can help autistic children when they become anxious with patience, discipline and love. Parents should ask for help and have the child evaluated. Its important to recognize behavior of autistic children so that you don't get frustrated and spank your child. Autistic children need to live as normal a life as possible.

Last fall I had no money and I knew that Christmas was coming and that my children would have no gifts. I prayed to God and, once again, He answered my prayers. He reminded me that nothing is too small for Him. He cares about every detail in our lives. Our local Boys and Girls club was approached by a church that had an outreach called The Christmas Project. They knew nothing of our circumstances other than we had no money and would not be having a Christmas. They gave us food for our stomachs and for our souls. They prayed over each person in our family during the months of preparation for our holiday delivery. They have continually blessed us over this year and I have made new friends. I'm so thankful for these people who showed a simple act of kindness and demonstrated so much love for us. My son looked so happy with all toys he would not have had otherwise. During Christmas, one of the best gifts was when the doctors were able to reduce his medication for epilepsy because he was doing so much better.

I believe it was because of the prayers. Prayers are powerful!

The More I Pursue You

Donna

Shock and denial were the emotions I felt when I found out I had stage four cancer of the tongue. Today I would like to share five miracles that I experienced along the way. I had been in post radiation and chemotherapy for ten months. Today, I am completely healed of cancer by the blood of Jesus.

THE FIRST MIRACLE ~ REVELATION.

I was totally healthy, or so I thought. I had no symptoms other than an enlarged lymph node. I am a sixty-one-year-old nurse and drug sales representative. During one of the doctor drop-offs, someone commented on the appearance of my lymph node.

They said, "You should have that checked out." I really felt great and did not think there was anything wrong with me. Still, I would go have it looked at, just in case.

I'm so thankful God guided me to wonderful doctors which led to my diagnosis and treatment that would eventually save my life. The miracle of my diagnosis was an astute doctor who took notice of my enlarged node when I was leaving the office for an unrelated problem. At that point he and I were not concerned . . . until I received the biopsy results, and it was determined that I had squamas cell carcinoma: stage four cancer.

The next nine weeks were incredibly difficult. The treatment was very aggressive and debilitating. I had nine weeks of chemo and radiation. On a scale of one to ten, it was a ten as far as adverse effects.

THE SECOND MIRACLE ~ THE GIFTS OF THE SPIRIT.

My husband, Dan, and I had never experienced anything like this before. The news of this cancer brought me to my knees. Dan suggested we attend a healing service. We came from a conservative church background and had never been to a service like this before. There were about 150 people in the room. At one point, the pastor said over the microphone, "Does anyone have arthritis? Does someone here need healing for their lower back?" As he called out the different conditions, the people went forward to receive prayer and healing for these things. I just kept waiting and I said, "Oh Lord, I want to be called. I want to be called." And finally, the pastor said, "Does anyone here have cancer?" I raised my hand and yelled, "I do. I do!" I felt like I had won the door prize on Monty Hall's show.

Tears were streaming down my face. I opened my arms wide and said, "Holy Spirit come!" I was praying, open for anything. By the grace of God, I stand here today to tell you, no person touched me. I fell back as the power of the Holy Spirit rushed over me. I tried to get up quickly, but the people encouraged me to just lay back and receive. I am here to say these gifts of the Spirit are real. I did not need the physical form of God to believe He exists. Sure, I possess a strong faith in God, but the Holy Spirit is alive and so real.

By the way, as a result of this encounter with Holy Spirit, Dan and I had a surreal peace about the cancer. I knew God would heal me. I just did not know how. Would it be immediate? Or would I have to go through with this therapy? Would I have to walk through the suffering? Without the suffering I wonder what my testimony would be?

I put all my trust in Him.

THE THIRD MIRACLE ~ ANSWERED PRAYER.

I am extremely claustrophobic. If God had to pick one thing that would absolutely bring me to my knees, it would be to put me in a confined space. During the radiation treatment there is a process that requires a tight mask that is fitted and molded to my face. The mask was so tight and covered my head and neck. It was bolted to the table so that I could not move.

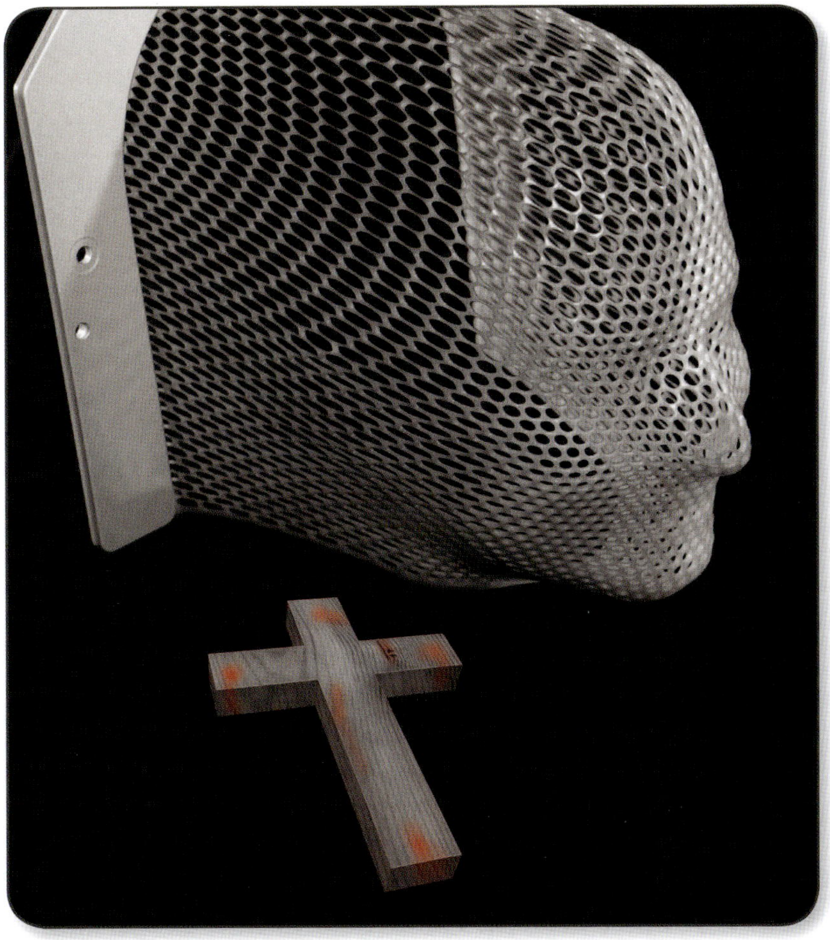

When they removed the mask, I would sigh with relief knowing my treatment time was over. Sometimes there was blood in the mask because it was so tight. I wanted to hold someone's hand. But they told me, "Oh Donna, you're going through radiation." So instead, I held tightly to a wooden cross that fit in the palm of my hand. With that cross, I felt the comfort of Jesus.

Before each therapy session, I would search through my bag like a baby looking for her pacifier. This wooden cross bore my fear, my anxiety and my claustrophobia. Jesus was ever present. He gave me peace, acceptance and endurance. This is a miracle if you know just how claustrophobic I am. At the end, my attitude was, "Bring it on. Bring It On!" I developed a strong attitude. Jesus was with me. I was not alone. He is real, so loving, and so personal.

THE FOURTH MIRACLE ~ THE LORD'S WORK.

I shouted really angrily, "If I have to go through this suffering, USE ME!" You promised me not one tear would be lost. During the time of radiation and treatments taking such a toll, people would come to my home to encourage us and pray. You can't imagine how I looked or felt. My face and shoulders were burned severely by the radiation. I looked like I had been dipped in hot oil. Later, even the nurses in the chemo room said, "Donna, when you walked in all we could do was close our eyes and begin to pray." I said, "Oh Lord, thank you for making me a sacrificial lamb, that my body would inspire people to immediately pray after looking upon my condition. I said, "Thank You, God, that you would use me in this way."

One couple that came to the house to pray for me was Jerry and Kat. Jerry pointed out that he had an enlarged lymph node identical to mine, and I encouraged him to follow up with his doctor. Indeed, it turned out to be cancer. It is so miraculous that God is bringing to me so many people from everywhere. Can you imagine? People with cancer were coming to me. And, not just any cancer — cancer of the tongue and throat. Go figure. I am just His servant. I don't even have to worry about what I am supposed to do tomorrow, or where I am supposed to go. God brings them to me.

THE FIFTH MIRACLE ~ THE REVELATION THAT ILLNESS IS A BLESSING.

Through this illness, I am able to share my faith in God. I have suffered in really adverse situations. No pain, no testimony! There is always joy. The joy of the Lord is my strength. He is very much alive. I am not afraid of death. "Death, where is thy sting?" You have no power over me, because

I have a wonderful home in heaven with my eternal Father. I imagine when I meet my Lord, I'll say, "Lord? Why me?" I imagine He'll say, "Why not you…my beloved? Why not you?"

Therefore we do not lose heart. Though outwardly we are wasting away,
yet inwardly we are being renewed day by day.
For our light and momentary troubles are achieving for us an eternal glory
that far outweighs them all. So we fix our eyes not on what is seen,
but on what is unseen. For what is seen is temporary,
but what is unseen is eternal.
1 Corinthians 14:16-18 NIV

My blog site: www.donnashealingjourney.blogspot.com

Standing Stone

Testify

Jesus Christ is the same yesterday and today and forever.
Hebrews 13:8b NIV

Every record of what God has done in generations past is a promise of what He will do again in our lives, because Jesus never changes. His love for us never changes. His desire for us to know Him, walk with Him, believe Him and to trust Him never changes.

Off Course

Pancho

If you sail a boat to Hawaii
and you steer just one degree
off course, by the time you near
your course destination you
would, in fact, be hundreds of
miles out of sight of land
and lost at sea.

As a young boy, Pancho began a love of the stars and all their glory. Growing up at the beach he spent countless hours enjoying surfing and sailing. Later he went on to get a degree in celestial navigation, which he used racing yachts around the world. He often looked up into the stars and wondered who was in control of the universe, but at that point he held the world in his own hands. He believed he was the captain of his own life.

indulging in every **reckless** temptation

This thinking worked well for him as a young adult. He pursued all his personal goals, believing his life was rich and full. Although he attained worldly success in many areas, deep down he knew it was self-serving. Still he pressed on, living without boundaries, indulging in every reckless temptation with the goal of living for the moment. And yet he was not content! What was missing? He had lost his moral compass.

Where once the very stars of the heavens lit up his life, he was consumed with darkness! Pancho felt off course, but did not know why or how to get back on course. His marriage was on the rocks and headed for divorce. He was alone, broken and lost, separated from his children and the people he learned that in order to remain on course, he must daily read the words of God in the Bible to re-calibrate his compass and heart, or he slowly drifts away from the true direction God intended for him.

Passionate about where he is going in life and who guides his ship, he has just one deep question… and the answers would come, not from the stars in the sky, but from his Lord.

Pancho asks in amazement, "Why had I not learned more about Jesus at an earlier period in my life? Why did I not understand what God wanted from me and for me? Why?'

The Bible says,

"For the earth will be filled with the knowledge of the glory of the Lord, as the waters cover the sea."
Habakkuk 2:14 NIV

RAISED FROM THE DEAD

Marian

To God be the Glory! I write this as a witness to His great healing power, His mercy, His love and His grace. This testimony is not about me. It is about the great and mighty God of the universe who has given me back the precious gift of life. I don't really know why God spared my life but I do know His purpose for me has not yet been fulfilled. All honor, all glory, all praise and thanksgiving to Him.

It was at a Christian women's retreat on a Sunday morning, October 12, 2008, that I suddenly collapsed with no dizziness, no weakness, no warning whatsoever. My long-time friend who was sitting beside me immediately called 911.

Two of God's angel nurses, Talar and Louise, were at my side in seconds and began CPR. My breathing was very shallow; there was no heartbeat or pulse; I was dead.

Moments later our pastor's wife called our church and they began to pray. I was told that many of the women at the retreat were on their faces praying to God that I would return to life.

The power of the Holy Spirit filled the room. The prayers of the saints were being answered although they did not realize this was happening for there were still no signs of life…no heartbeat, no pulse. After some time the church was called for the second time to let them know I had died.

Talar and Louise were led by the power of the Holy Spirit and never stopped administering CPR. It appeared hopeless but they did not give up. God's plan suddenly began to unfold. After approximately fifteen minutes they discovered a heartbeat. I can only imagine what went on in that retreat room after the announcement…praises, thank you and all the glory being given to God.

The third phone call to the church informed the entire Sunday congregation that I was alive. What a miracle!

I knew nothing about what had happened. I did not gain consciousness until the fourth day. On my way to Fallbrook Hospital via ambulance I was hardly able to breathe, even with life support. The heartbeat and the pulse were very weak. A call was made to my

JUST AS I AM

Louise

How do I fit in? Where can I serve in the body of Christ? I want answers! What is my purpose? Louise has been a nurse in the medical profession for many years. Yet, these are the feelings and thoughts she had when she went to a women's retreat. All weekend she had prayed that God would answer her prayers. He, of course, met her right where she was and answered every need.

Her testimony…

Sunday morning, in closing for our women's retreat, we gathered for live music and fellowship. This was a time to share warm fuzzies and inspirations and personal revelations

husband, Paul. When he arrived at the hospital, the attending physician told him there was very little hope that I would survive and that he should call the family, which he did. They were at the hospital within hours.

Previously, I had given my primary physician an advanced medical directive, which stated, "no life support." At the hospital they tried to take out the breathing tubes twice. I was unable to breathe on my own both times. In reference to the directive, they asked if they should discontinue the life support. My husband responded, "No, definitely not at this time." When they pulled the breathing tubes out on the fourth day I was able to breathe on my own and shortly thereafter regained consciousness. Glory to God!

of the things that had taken place over the weekend. Marian shared about total surrender to the Holy Spirit. My thoughts began to wander.

What I perceived when I looked around the room was beautiful women without an ounce of fat on their bodies. Their husbands, I imagined, were perfect, strong Christian men. They probably had perfect, well-behaved children and still managed to volunteer at every church event. I knew they must all be creative, well organized, and kept immaculate houses. These were the absurd thoughts that seeped into my mind. I compared myself inaccurately to others as I saw only terrible flaws and imperfections in myself. I was insecure. I knew God loved me, but it seemed I had no confidence or strength in that. I made a decision to trust in the Lord and prayed for faith.

As I was pondering these thoughts, Marian had already returned to her seat. Suddenly, someone called to me. Will you look at Marian? The look on her face clearly said to get to Marian in a hurry. I jumped up and went to Marian's side. She was seated in a chair. Her eyes were rolled back and she was not breathing. Talar and I positioned her on the floor. The room filled with shock and fear. Immediately I felt a supernatural peace.

God has a plan and purpose for everything that happens in our lives. He uses circumstances to bring about His divine will. Being conscious, I had many questions about what had happened. I thanked the Lord for the miracle of life and thought about some things that had preceded my death. At that time I became aware of how He used many people to bring about my coming back to life.

He did answer my prayers but in a *very unexpected* way!

When I was at the retreat I had arranged to ride home with friends on Saturday night after one of them, Minka, spoke to the women at the retreat on "The power of the Holy Spirit." Shortly after she spoke, she collapsed. 911 was called and she was admitted to the hospital for the night. As I had no ride home on Saturday night I stayed at the retreat hotel. Had I gone home on Saturday night as planned, and the incident occurred in my home,

Even though people were shouting directions, I was perfectly focused and God gave me the ability to clearly see Marian and know the action we were to take. With no pulse, we began CPR. The exact positioning and action flowed from my body. Even though I had never done CPR outside the hospital, Talar and I made a perfect team. I remembered how to check for proper compressions and ventilation. It felt easy and effortless. A peace that passes all understanding permeated my soul and the crowd had no influence on my performance.

Thanks be to the Living King. Only He could do that. Order my steps in this way. Put me right where I was supposed to be, using the gifts that He alone has given me to serve others. It was a miracle. A Life was saved.

Today, I stand firm in the assurance that I'm fearfully and wonderfully made in His image, able to do all things through Christ who strengthens me.

I do belong, just as I am, perfect in Him.

my husband would not have been strong enough to give me CPR since he was still recovering from pneumonia. Again, God's intervention and His plan fulfilled.

The next thing that came to my mind was that about a month before the retreat I was praying and asking God to use me, particularly in sharing my faith with others. He did answer my prayers, but in a very unexpected way.

Only God knows why this miracle took place. I do believe that His purpose for me personally was to increase my faith and to draw me closer to Him, to make me more dependent on Him, and to use me. Many came to visit me after my recuperation period and told me how touched they were at what God had done and how their faith had grown because of it.

On Friday, two days before I collapsed, I was chitchatting with someone when out of the blue I said, "I'm going to the hospital." I don't know why I said those words but in retrospect I believe the Holy Spirit was preparing me for what was to happen.

AN OPEN DOOR

Talar

I had not been to a retreat in 6 years. This year I really needed to hear from the Lord. I said to God, "I will go to this retreat if you will please just talk to me and let me know if I am supposed to pursue my dream of becoming a nurse." In the past few years so many people had told me to give up on my dreams. Even some close friends and family said things like, "Maybe God doesn't want you to be a nurse." But, ever since I finished school in Iraq, I believed that God wanted me to serve Him in this way. I felt discouraged and I was questioning God.

Before I left the hospital, the doctor told me how amazed he was that I made it, that very few come back to life from cardiac arrest. He also told me that in giving CPR almost always the ribs are broken. Mine were not. My thoughts were of Jesus on the cross…no broken bones.

My story is one of praise and thanksgiving to my heavenly Father who gave me back the precious gift of life, and to my family, friends and church who prayed so diligently and faithfully for me during my time of need. A special thank you to God's angels, Talar and Louise, who never gave up and continued CPR. God truly used them as instruments of life.

In conclusion, this miracle has made me know without a doubt that:

God answers prayer.

He is the God of miracles and that they are happening today.

He is the same today, yesterday and tomorrow.

The main theme of the retreat that weekend was the Holy Spirit. I kept praying to God, what do you want me to do? On Sunday morning, Marian got up and shared about trusting in the Lord and surrendering. I was sitting next to a friend who kept elbowing me saying, "Talar, listen to what Marian is saying. You need to trust God with everything and let the Holy Spirit speak to you, because He will!"

As I was contemplating what my friend said, they introduced another speaker. I was meditating over and over again what it means to give it all up to God. A few minutes later, Marian lost consciousness. Someone called me to help. I was going through this process in my mind. I know CPR, but I am not a licensed nurse here in California. I have only been a nurse in my home country. I know that God gave me the ability to perform CPR. What should I do? God help me! It seemed like an eternity as thoughts raced in my mind, but God was swift and threw me right into action.

I moved in faith to help Marian. I kept praying over her as we worked to bring her back to life. We continued to breathe for her and compress her for at least 15 minutes! I was praying the entire time. While I was praying, I clearly heard the Lord tell me, "I gifted you as

We don't know His plan or purpose, but He will use us if only we will ask Him.

Every moment of our lives is a gift from Him.

a nurse." God did a miracle. Through another friend and nurse, Louise, and I, He raised Marian from the dead! As for me, He fulfilled the dreams that He put in my heart. God gave me the power and the ability, the courage to take my nursing test and pass. I received the answers to the questions I had at the beginning of this weekend retreat. Now I knew for certain that God had a plan for me and I am fulfilling that plan! I now serve the Lord as a hospice nurse and rejoice that He gave me such a rewarding place in His kingdom here on earth.

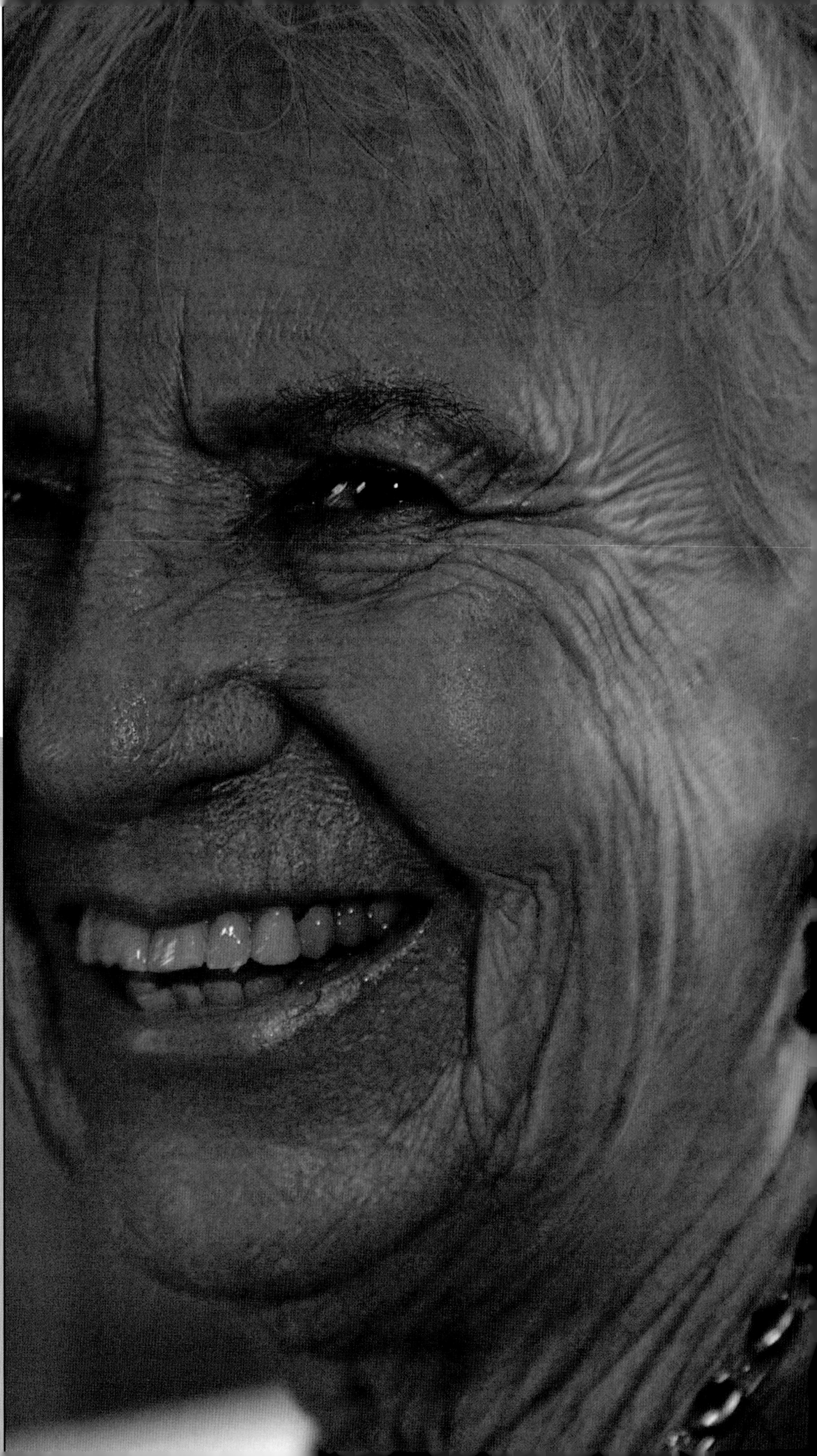

The Ministry of Great Sorrow

Karen

I evolved from a life of pain into a woman of victory. This hope I describe to you is not intended for pity or sadness. The story is to encourage you to move forward in whatever burden or struggle you are facing. You see, courage has a "ripple effect." You may think what you say and do doesn't make a difference, but it does. I can choose to walk forward; I can choose to thrive, and this was my journey.

A Life Undone

One quiet afternoon, my husband, Bob, walked into the house and sat me down. He told me that he had been having an affair for almost a year and would be leaving our family. He then told our four sons the same. This was the person I trusted most in the entire world. We had been married almost thirty years and now Bob tells me he had been secretly meeting with a married woman. His decision to pursue this affair broke my heart!

He walked out the door and left us behind. My four sons and I were in shock. We never imagined this could happen to us.

Some days it felt as if there was not enough paper to write down all of the things I went through. This experience has been the hardest thing I have ever had to do, so painful, I could not have imagined this kind of grief existed.

C.S. Lewis gave me a new perspective on grief that I'd like to share.

> "The death (or betrayal) of a beloved is an amputation..." "There are moments, most unexpectedly, when something inside me tries to assure me that I don't really mind so much, this grief, not so very much, after all. Love is not the whole person's life. I've got plenty of what are called resources. People get over these things. Come on now, I'm not doing so badly. One is ashamed to listen to this voice, but it seems for a little while to be making a good case. Then comes a sudden jab of red-hot memories and all of the 'common-sense' vanishes like an ant in the mouth an enormous furnace."

The Journey

Knowing I needed help I went to Colorado for intensive counseling at a ministry called Restoring the Soul. For weeks I met with the founder of the ministry in what he calls Soul Care Intensives. God used Michael, a devoted and passionate servant, in my life in such a powerful way. I detailed in my journal all of the counseling sessions recording each praise, each healing, and every step taken. Reading those journals is like listening to a symphony; all the tears and prayers came together to make an incredible music of praise!

I can grieve if I need to, but my **wounds** or my **feelings** do not **define** me.

I recognized I needed healing from the wounds of my past. I grew up as a sweet little girl who just wanted someone to love her. During counseling I faced all the fears I had of being hurt, abandoned and alone.

I beheld the Lord in the dark, wounded places and was given freedom. I came to accept my total brokenness facing rejection, humiliation and finally dying to myself. I let go of the dream of a lifetime with the man that I love and, as hard as it was, I forgave him, as well as myself. And after all that rejection, guess what? During this process, I discovered how much God really loves me.

One of the entries in my journal read:

> ***"Again! Again! I am in a place of laying down my need to control, convince and appeal to Bob that we can recover from this. It is a roller coaster of ups and downs for myself with this behavior. I can fight what is happening, or I can come into agreement with the circumstances of my life and allow God to work. Some days I feel like a two-year-old swinging my fists into the air, throwing a temper tantrum and screaming, "Nooooooo!!!" to the Lord, that I do not want to do this. When I fight, I am so BROKEN. When I SURRENDER, I am so FILLED. God comes and pours into me. He is the God of boundless resources. The only limit is ME."***

During my stays in Colorado I experienced some of the most intimate moments with my Lord. One day, in an audible voice He said to me, "Rest, rest, My Daughter; rest, stop fighting. Now rest." Another day I heard, "Embrace your sorrow. This is your life." My heart wept the day I heard God say to me: "The reason that I want to heal you is because your broken heart prevents you from knowing My love for you, Karen."

Surrender

Each visit, the Lord made it very clear why I was there. I was to take one step forward every time. God showed me some amazing things. One time, the Lord began a healing of the intense grief in my heart. This sorrow was a pain worse than if my husband had died. The betrayal and the loss of my world intensified the sadness. What was normal for me and my boys had changed forever. My counselor, Michael, told me: "The question of our life is not whether we surrender, but who we will surrender to."

I resolved to surrender to my Abba Father the rest of my life.

In my journal that month I wrote:

> ***The act of living is different than it ever has been before. After this week, it feels like my life alone is beginning to become my reality. I say beginning, because I have a long way to go. But this week has brought me to a place to begin and thrive on that journey. I have cried more tears than could fit in a bottle, but I know God is storing them for me and counts every one of them. I can grieve if I need to, but my wounds or my feelings do not define me. Yet, God has brought me great joy in this realization! There is a sense of wonder in me, an expectation of God's covering, a release of my grasp on trying to change things, that my life will be good and I will be happy, despite all that has gone on over the last year.***

Many times I wanted it all to go away, this mess of my life. Or I wanted to think that it was not true, all that was happening to the boys and me. But this is my life! Once I accepted the reality of it God was able to bring me to a different place in my heart. I could not have found freedom without seeing His perspective.

I have found that when we come into agreement with Him, our minds become powerful tools in God's hands. My understanding of this reality in my life determines what I think and how I live. I need to live my life knowing with all certainty that God has a wonderful future for me, whether that is with my husband or not. God is so good to me and I am so grateful for His provision, grace and love for me. I trust in the Lord and hold tight to the promises He has given me.

Sometimes it is necessary for God to keep us in the circumstances and things of our life that are unseen. He wants to bring us to the end of our own strength and let us see that without Him we are helpless. I have to trust that my life has some kind of direction, meaning, or a picture of my future. He is keeping me in things that are unseen and I am leaving it all up to Him.

"While we do not look at things which are seen, but at things which are not seen.
For the things which are seen are temporary, but the things which are not seen are eternal."
2 Corinthians 4:18 NIV

I thank God that my season of great sorrow has become a symphony of praise. God has used many wonderful people to encourage and pray for me along the way. Over the past two years, He has strengthened and equipped me to be the head of my household. He has carried me through my studies as I work toward a degree in Psychology. Today my boys and I live in a new home. I stand at the doorway looking out wondering what God has for my future, anticipating how He will use my testimony to serve others. I'm eternally grateful that He has taken my ashes and turned them into beauty.

Walking Through Fires

Jeff

In April, I was working on the Sierra Madre fire. It was an early-season fire that threatened surrounding structures. As a fire captain I normally run inmate hand crews. This time I happened to be on an engine. While fighting this fire I started feeling sick with a cough that wouldn't stop. We worked on controlling the fire for three or four days. When that was done I went directly to a twenty-four-hour clinic to hopefully get some antibiotics to make the cough go away. The doctor gave me a prescription. She also ordered a chest x-ray that would change the next fifteen months of my life.

My wife, Jill, reminded me that I had been coughing several months before with bronchitis and the cough never really left me. So, then, it was a done deal. I had the chest x-ray and a few days later was back at work. I never heard anything from the doctor about my x-ray and I was feeling better. So, like any other person, I didn't give it a lot of thought. Hey, no news is good news!

That morning, I took the crew on a hike and when I got back my wife called and said they found something in my lungs. The doctor wanted me to see a pulmonary specialist and have a CAT scan.

Instead of FIGHTING fires I began a fight for MY LIFE

I told my boss what was going on. I had to wait for relief before I could leave. I had some time to kill while I waited, so I called my good friend. He had been my friend since third grade and is also my brother-in-law. I told him what was going on and I said, "I do not want to go through this crap again!"

Nine years ago I had a benign brain tumor the size of a tennis ball. That happened right before my wedding. Not fun, but I thought, here we go again. Instead of fighting fires, I began a fight for my life. I made an appointment with my doctor who had scheduled a CAT scan that would give more details than the x-ray. The doctor said the spot on my lung was serious and could be anything from pneumonia to the worst…cancer. These doctors don't mess around! They don't want to tell you anything that might give you false hope. Thankfully, I had friends and family in my life that spoke words of hope and encouragement. One good friend said to me, "Jeff, God told me that everything is going to be okay." And then he prayed for me.

The next few weeks took me through various tests, which included a lung biopsy. This one scared me. I knew that to do the biopsy they would have to puncture my lung. Immediately I thought of all the complications that could happen! Being a fireman, I have seen people with punctured lungs, chest tubes and struggling to breathe. It did not look fun. During the procedure I was praying and five separate times God said to me, "Jeff, everything is going to be okay"

Contrary to what God told me the doctor put it to me bluntly, "I'm sorry, Jeff, it does not look good. You have stage four lung cancer." He told me he had consulted with an oncologist and wanted me to see him ASAP. My mind went racing a million miles an hour thinking of what was going to happen to my wife, my two boys and the rest of my life. I felt horrible for my family. I felt I had let them down and would be putting them through all of this again. About one thing I was confident: I knew I would be going to heaven! But, what to do until then?

Jill and I began to cry out for help. That night our pastor, friends and family came to our house. They laid hands on me and prayed for healing in my body. The room was overwhelmed with emotions. Right then I made a decision to let go, to really give this cancer to God and let him deal with it. God is in control. So I was off work until further notice. This was a new thing for me. I loved being a firefighter but now that I had mandatory time off, I realized that I had put work first. I took this time as a free pass to enjoy my family and friends and live every moment of life to the fullest. Over the next couple of months I received a lot of chemo and a lot of prayer. So many friends prayed and even shaved their heads in support. Even after all the chemo, I never lost any hair. We all enjoyed God's sense of humor!

Those good friends laid their hands on me and we prayed that God would take all my burdens. From that moment on, for the most part, I was at a peace. Any time and any place I could get prayer, I would.

Twelve weeks of chemo and all the waiting aside, I went in for my first PET scan. I was not scared. I had ambitions of being totally healed. After the scan, both techs came in and stated that they did not see any obvious signs of any tumors or cancer. They, of course, put out the disclaimer that they are just techs and the radiologist can see a whole lot more in these pictures. I was excited to hear that! These guys had remembered me from my earlier PET scans and thought that I had the most amount of cancer they had ever seen in a picture! Now what they were looking for did not exist. I gave God the glory!

I had my follow-up appointment with my oncologist. He said we had really good results from the chemo and that 98% of the cancer was gone! I said Amen! My doctor's plan was to go for 100% cancer free. He decided to continue with chemo and radiation. I was still relying on God. I held on to one scripture throughout this struggle,

"Because he loves me," says the LORD, "I will rescue him;
I will protect him, for he acknowledges my name.
He will call upon me, and I will answer him;
I will be with him in trouble, I will deliver him and honor him.
With long life will I satisfy him and show him my salvation."
Psalm 91:14-16 NIV

This struggle with cancer had lasted almost a year. I do love God and he has rescued me. He has delivered me. All was confirmed when I heard my doctor declare, "Jeff, there is NO cancer!" Again, I give ALL the glory to God! He is so awesome! I now live cancer free. I do not know why God healed me specifically. I met two other guys who were diagnosed around the same time as me, who had families with children, and they both passed away. One of them was a Christian brother. I guess if God wants me to know, I will find out in heaven some day.

I believe God wants to use me and I wait patiently so see what He has in store for me. For now I share my story whenever possible and tell people to have hope and to pray. Pray, pray, pray like they never have before and receive prayer any time they can.

That kind of sums it all up. I'm back working as a fire captain and doing the same thing any other man would if he had seen his life flash before him. I have a new creed: God first, family second, and then work. I know not to make work my idol anymore. I have been a Christian a long time. As God walks alongside me, these fires refine me.

Standing Stone

Testify

Anyone who believes in the Son of God has this testimony in his heart.
1 John 5:10 NIV

The testimonies of God are the tools that equip us to walk in our purposes to demonstrate what He is like through the miraculous. These testimonies create an expectation in our hearts for God's ways to be manifested in our lives.

Crazy Making

Aubrey

My mom and I were so close growing up. She was more than a mother; she was my friend, that is, until I was 19, when things started to change between us. She befriended a woman we'll call Jane, who was involved in a religious cult and became a big influence in her life. We did not know then how much power this person would have over my mother's future. Everyone but my mom could see how destructive this woman was, leading her down the wrong path. Since I did not agree with Mom's choices, she turned her back on me and everything I believed in as a Christian woman. Suddenly, she was cold and distant. She was no longer the fun-loving, spirited mother, and she severed her relationships with my dad, my brother and I.

During that time, I had been dating Donovan and leaned heavily on him for support. Turning to the Lord we found comfort and soon began to plan one of the biggest days in a woman's life: our wedding day! By the end of that year we were to be married. I would end up being a bride without my mom standing beside me. I was devastated. Donovan and I kept our focus on God and it was He who provided a wonderful woman to stand in my mother's place for this special occasion. With my friend Kat helping me, we did all the mother-daughter things that go into planning a wedding. We had so much fun, but deep down I ached for my mom. It was one of the hardest times in my life.

Three years later our first baby, Dylan, was born. Donovan and I were thrilled and embraced parenthood with joy and excitement. Again, my mom was not there to share in our happiness. This was her firstborn grandchild.

Throughout the pregnancy I could not understand why my mother chose the beliefs of a cult over a relationship with me.

As Dylan was growing up, I was overwhelmed with confusion. I could not in a million years think of abandoning my son like my mom had done with me! It just wasn't right. That's not what mothers do. For many years, I went to counseling trying to cope with my feelings of rejection and abandonment. I prayed for God to open her eyes to the truth. Through all the pain, I still had hope that one day she would return.

In October of 2008 that day would come! A dear friend called and told me she saw my mom at a post wedding party for a couple that had recently married. I was shocked to learn the person they were honoring was the daughter of my mom's cult leader! Feeling angry and heart-broken I immediately text-messaged my mom: "How dare you honor that woman's daughter when you didn't want any part of my wedding, your one and only daughter."

Two hours later my mom called. When I saw her name on my phone I panicked! We had not talked in such a long time! I refused to pick it up but she kept calling back. Over and over the phone rang and rang until finally I took the call. She said, "Hi Aubrey, do you want to talk?" What could I say after so many years of separation?

On one hand I was angry and upset; on the other I was vulnerable and afraid. This turmoil rolled around inside as I struggled for what to say. Beaten down from the absence of my mother's love I told her, "Mom, you have really hurt me and I don't understand why. I am so tired of you not being there for me." Then, my heart stopped and my jaw hit the floor. I couldn't believe the words came out of her mouth. "Aubrey, I've missed you and want to be in your life again." Was I dreaming?

She said she realized how much pain she had caused. We made plans to meet at the harbor the next day to talk. I was nervous knowing she was still involved in the cult and didn't want to get my hopes up.

There by the water we spent hours talking. Trying to understand, I asked her many questions, and as we spoke about the past we both cried. On my way home, I had this feeling she had one foot in the cult and one foot out. So much time had passed between us that it was hard to catch up in just one visit.

I made the decision I WAS NOT GOING to lose her *again*

Donovan and I decided to invite her over for dinner the next night and she accepted. It went well, though it was awkward, to say the least. During the following week we would spend a lot of time talking and sharing our hearts with one another. Dylan was getting to know his Gamma and I could tell it touched her in a deep way.

The Roller Coaster

Then came Friday morning when my phone rang. Mom called, wanting to speak face to face. Being in a hurry to get to work, I asked her what was up. Something in the tone of her voice disturbed me. Trying to prepare for the worst, I braced myself emotionally. "Aubrey, I think I've made a mistake and I cannot do this. I don't believe it's possible to reconcile this relationship!"

I crumbled, falling to the floor in disbelief as my heart sank within me. Again, I was devastated. In anguish I cried out to God, knowing I could not live like this anymore. She was making me crazy! Indignation came over me from the bottom of my soul and I made the decision I was not going to lose her again! I knew what I had to do! I put on the full armor of God (Eph. 6: 11) and stood my ground!

Thank God Donovan was home that morning. He instantly began praying. He told me to tell her about the fruit of the Spirit and how none of them were apparent in her life: joy, peace, kindness....(Gal. 5:22-23)

I reminded my mother how miserable she had been and how the leader of the cult had brainwashed her. I encouraged her not to listen to anything Jane would say. She was quiet but in the end she said, "I need more time to think about this." I told her, "If you walk away now it will have to be forever, because I won't go through this again." I hung up thinking, this is it! I might never talk to my mom again. I was a wreck.

I had to go to work, and yet I wasn't physically able to put one foot in front of the other. I was crying so hard it was as if someone had knocked the wind right out of me. Reluctantly I dragged myself into the office. I thank God I was there by myself! Later my dad stopped by to comfort me.

Just a few hours had passed when I heard my cell phone ring. I panicked! The caller ID read: Mom's cell. What was she doing calling me? I couldn't take any more insanity! I chose not to answer it. She called again and again. Finally, she left a message.

She said she realized that everything I said on the phone before was true. My mom declared she was done with the cult for good! She begged my forgiveness and asked for patience. Mom announced she was cutting off all relationship with Jane!

It was unbelievable. When I called her back she sounded like a different person. This coaster ride had to come to an end right now! Her change of mind had to be set in stone. She had to own up to all the hurt she'd put us through. She came over that night and we talked, crying for what seemed like hours on end. It was painful trying to make up for lost time. The following Sunday she joined our family at church. In faith, I prayed her heart would be truly changed and her mind set free, that some day she would discover the liberty she has in Christ.

It's been over a year since my mom and I have reconciled. Let me tell you, it's been great! God has blessed Donovan and I. We found out in December 2008 that we were going to have twins! This pregnancy would be so different, as my mom was by my side. God gave us back more joy than we had ever known. He made up for all the years that had been lost. During the past six years God had continually given me slivers of hope to hold on to. I'm so grateful we're on the other side of it now. To God be the glory!

July 31st, twins Sydney and Ryan were born, and my mom was there every step of the way. To Him be all the Glory!

My Greatest Mistake

Kathy

Dear Aubrey and Brian,

Before I try to answer any of your questions or concerns, first let me say that I live daily with the shame of how much I have hurt my two children, something I vowed I would never do. I cannot undo what I have done; I can only beg forgiveness and ask that you will allow me to be a part of your lives again. Sometimes I look back on what happened and I can't believe it myself. If I could erase the past I would do it in a heartbeat, because the daily regret is sometimes too much to bear. I understand that you would have an insulation layer around yourself. I am ashamed that I am responsible for even a small part of that. I understand that I should be on your list of people you don't trust, however I would like to someday have my name removed from that list permanently! I will do whatever it takes to make that happen. You just tell me what it is you need to talk about and I will talk honestly and openly. It might not always make sense to the two of you. You might think I was half (no, completely) out of my mind, but I will talk to you both about anything. You are my children.

Brian, for you, my son, I'm glad that you and Julie have a wonderful relationship and she is the focus of your life! As you have said, she is a sure thing for you and I know you are a sure thing for her.

Aubrey, I'm thankful God has raised you up into a beautiful young woman and that he gave you an awesome husband to come alongside in my absence.

I'm happy that both of my children have spouses who truly love them. That is how a marriage should be. Saying "I'm sorry" is not going to fix what I have done, however it does have to be said. It expresses regret and I have an extreme amount of regret for hurting you. I do take responsibility for what I've done. It is not an easy thing to explain in writing. I don't want to make excuses. I can only express how it came about. You were right when you said I've had a rough life. Both of you knew I was going through an awful time in my own marriage. I was literally in a state of fear and depression. With [Jane], she was more than a friend. She became my spiritual leader. I felt unconditional love, acceptance and attention. She was the only one that was listening to me.

The counseling became controlling and I secluded myself from everyone I knew and loved. It got to the point where the isolation made me an open target for brainwashing.

I was confused and wanting spiritual answers. [Jane] provided that as she manipulated Scripture into everything she told me to do, and I did it. With my own life so out of control, it seemed easier to let her make decisions. Because I was so vulnerable, I did what I was told, even to the point of disconnecting myself from my children thinking you would be better off, spiritually, in the long run.

I know how utterly ridiculous this sounds because even I now look back and think, "How could I ever have been so stupid and gullible to allow someone to control and manipulate my life, especially when it came to my children?" What a fool! My Son and Daughter, I hope you find it in your hearts to someday truly forgive me. Allow me to speak with you so that I can answer any questions. This letter is only a very small part of everything that led up to the greatest mistake of my life.

I love you. I always have and I always will.
Your Mom

The Third Day

Julio

My name is Julio and I would like to share with you part of my life story before I came to know Jesus Christ, and I will share with you my testimony, my new life in Christ, King of all honor and glory.

Several years ago my walk in this life was very difficult. Haughtiness, pride, jealousy, aggressiveness, false pleasures and drugs of this world ruled my life. I converted my home into what you would call a "living hell." There was a void in my heart. I would wake up every morning with an aching soul. I was so tired of the same

I felt the HOLY GHOST *invading* my life ...

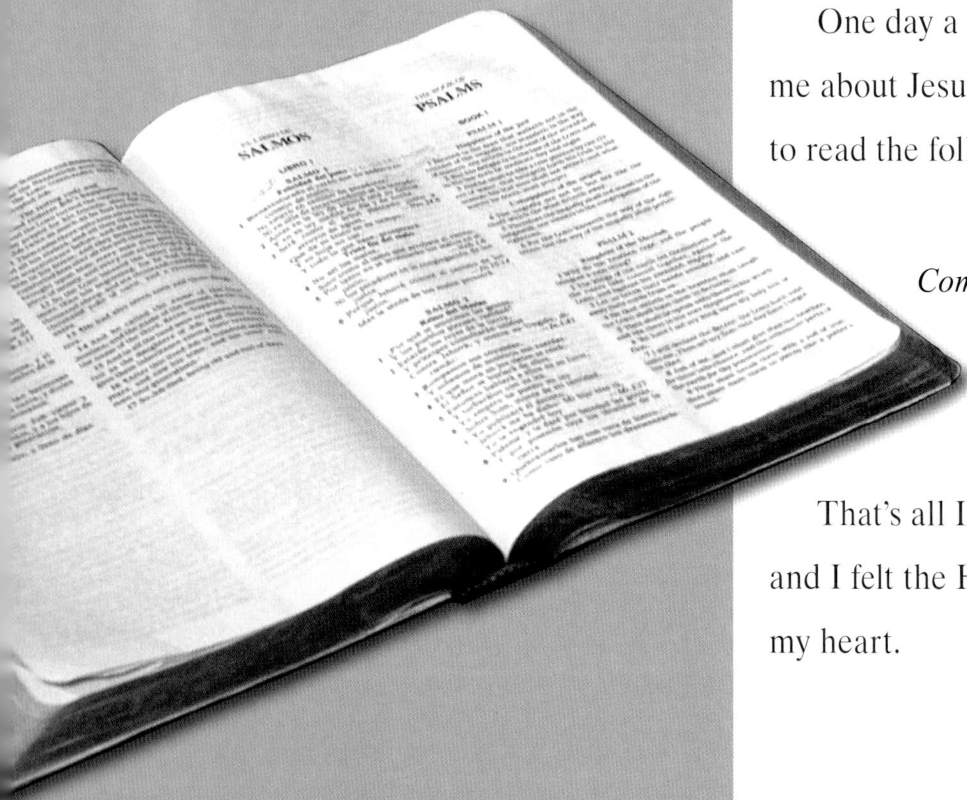

routine and problems, stress, yelling and fighting with my family at home. All of these problems caused a decline in my health. I started having stomach issues, acid reflux and ulcers.

I was anxious and depressed. All these symptoms slowly and surely started consuming my life.

Due to my agitated lifestyle I suffered from insomnia for three years. During those years I took every possible medication there is for all my stomach problems. I took Paxil for depression and to help keep me relaxed during the day. For insomnia I took Ambien. At this point in my life I started having suicidal thoughts. Twice I tried to commit suicide by hanging myself in the garage at the apartment where I used to live. Why I could not go through with it is something that I don't even know myself. Every time I intended to take my own life I would end up crying uncontrollably. I just could not stop.

One day a light of hope came to my life. A man began to talk to me about Jesus Christ. He placed a Bible in my hands and asked me to read the following scripture:

Come to me, all you who are weary and burdened,
and I will give you rest.
Matthew 11:28 NIV

That's all I was able to read for my hand started trembling and I felt the Holy Ghost invading my life and filling that void in my heart.

During the same week I went to two church services. God healed me. No more Paxil, no more Ambien. No more drugs for my stomach! Now my life is completely different with my wife, my children and with every person that surrounds my life. God takes care of those who love Him.

One night, several weeks later, I was sleeping and all of a sudden I woke up because I could not breathe. I had no strength to get up. I felt my body very heavy and numb. I could not move. I could hear my family talking in the living room but I could not call to them. Fortunately my wife walked into the bedroom and with great difficulty I was able to tell her that I did not feel well. Right away she called 911. The next thing I remember is being in the emergency room at the hospital. I couldn't feel my left arm and leg. I had suffered a stroke.

The doctor's ordered more tests to determine the extent of damage to the brain. Then I saw a great number of people from our church outside the hospital room praying with my wife asking God to have mercy on me and to perform a healing miracle in my life. God heard our cry and answered our prayers. When the test results came back they showed no damage to the brain.

i felt something horrible and hot, very hot, leave my body exiting through my back.

The following day I started having an anxiety attack. I experienced an ugly feeling, something dark trying to take control of my mind. When this came upon me, my family recognized these symptoms from the past, depression and anxiety. They were fearful I would lose my mind and not recognize them. I was afraid to fall asleep, afraid that this dark spirit would not allow me to wake up again.

That afternoon, the pastor and his wife came to visit and he told me, "Brother Julio, do not be afraid. God is with you and we are going to pray. Our God that we serve is going to heal you for He is the Doctor of life and death." As the room filled with prayers of faith and the pastor laid hands on me, I felt something horrible and hot, very hot, leave my body exiting through my back. At that very moment the Lord Jesus Christ healed me and restored my peace and confidence once again.

The third day, after many tests, every result came back with positive, encouraging results and I was discharged from the hospital and able to go home. Later that afternoon a brother from church came to visit my hospital room and found the bed empty. He asked the nurse that was taking care of me, "Where is Julio?" She said, "Julio went home. There is nothing wrong with him — absolutely nothing. You all have a God who listens and answers your prayers. Julio has been healed!"

This is why I serve my God. He has given me an abundant life, peace everlasting, joy, patience and freedom to adore Him.

Awake, Oh Princess

Kalina

"Sleeper, awake! Rise from the dead, and Christ will shine on you."

My little sisters and I waited with childish anticipation for our fairy-tale dolls to come in the mail. Our mother had ordered them from the back of a cereal box: Sharon's was Cinderella, Lisa's was Snow White, and mine was Sleeping Beauty. I loved the story where the beautiful princess falls under an evil curse that can only be broken by a kiss of true love from the son of a king. Little did I know that one day I would have more in common with this sleeping princess than I imagined. But I am awake! Now I know that I am a princess that has been awakened from a deep, spiritual sleep to find such a sweet kiss from my first true love. He is my portion and I am His.

As a Christian, I had been going to church these past twenty years, even serving in the children's ministry. Did I love God? Indeed I did and I knew that He loved me, but over time I realized that there was something missing from my relationship with the God of the universe. I have always counted myself truly blessed despite any of the challenges that I have faced. I was fortunate to have married the man of my dreams and blessed with two amazing sons and a precious daughter. Together we have weathered through a few storms of life, which would have been impossible without God's amazing grace and mercy.

We know what it feels like to watch everything we own burn down to the ground in a firestorm, to be without a change of clothing or a place to live and see all of our camera equipment destroyed, the very tools of our trade. We would struggle to rebuild only to be challenged by other factors. God has seen me through the trials of almost losing my beautiful man to a rare disease, my young sons in a fatal car accident, and the discovery of a lump in my breast. That year I thought, little Gabrielle was the only one without a near death trauma, then I realized that she almost lost all of us! It was no coincidence her very name means God is my strength! Through everything God was drawing me nearer and dearer to Him as I learned from each experience a richer understanding of His great love.

I suppose that is what made me want even more of Him. The more I fell in love with Jesus the more I wanted to worship Him. This spiritual desire led me to take time off from church for a season. It was a desert experience as I wandered around searching for what was missing. This kingdom secret would be revealed to me when I discovered my children's godmother, Deena, was stricken with cancer. I ran straight to the Lord with such intensity, hardly believing it was possible. Deena was one of the godliest women I knew. Lord, please don't let this happen. Prior to that I never had a prayer closet, never had a prayer language and never knew that I was a princess of a royal priesthood who had fallen asleep under the veil of lies.

In the beginning I had a basic understanding of God's gifts and was grateful knowing that as a sinner I received His most precious gift of salvation through His Son, Jesus Christ. I took for granted all the creative talents and abilities God had given me as a mother, wife and encouraging friend and claimed them as my own. But the deeper gifts of the Spirit, no thank you. Those I pushed away denying that they were for me. Those gifts were covered in mystery and wrapped in the unknown, and that scared me beyond measure. Now, however, I was choosing to press forward spiritually in a way that I had never done before. I was seeking God's face with all of my heart, all of my soul, all of my mind. I was willing to accept ALL that He had for me without reservation.

Coming out of my wilderness experience I found myself at a new church and small group Bible study. One night I confessed to those in the group how frustrated I was with everyone trying to get me to plug in to one type of ministry or another, especially in the area of serving. My heart's burning desire was to worship Him completely, and as if in stark contrast I heard myself complain out loud about performing a simple act of hospitality venting, "I did not come here to bake cookies!"

A woman responded from across the room saying, "Sounds to me like you are trying to make up for lost time!" Relief swept over me as she had defined my condition. That's what I wanted, to make up for time lost in slumber these past 20 years! I wanted Him NOW more than ever. I needed to demonstrate to Him how much I loved Him in words that only He could understand. And this would become my love language to The Lord.

> And that which you ask for **YOUR FRIEND** you seek for **YOURSELF**

I had prayed with people over the years, but not like I was praying most recently with my new prayer partner, Nina. She used the Word of God mightily and prayed in the Spirit, meaning she prayed in tongues. I needed intense penetrating prayer and hearing Nina speak in tongues seemed far less bizarre as I ignored those fears clinging to every promise of God that flew out of her mouth like a sword from a sheath.

We often spent time praying over the phone. This morning she was going to pray with me for Deena and informed me that she was getting into her prayer spot. I did not know what that meant on

her end but I know what was happening on mine. I had been so worried and now I felt a stirring from deep within me. It was as though I was about to be taken away for the ride of my life. Everything had been building up to this point and I knew it!

Not having a prayer closet or anything resembling that, I stepped into my daughter's small, girly, slightly messy bedroom with my cell phone in hand. The air was thick; it was electrifying, closing the door behind me knowing somehow I was not alone. What happened next mere words cannot adequately express, but together we washed my friend in the Word of God. Inside her body and outside aligning every cell with the Word, Nina prayed so hard and so fast that it would have been impossible to transcribe.

I tried to write it all down for Deena's sake, wanting her to know the very words that were being spoken over her. Crying out loud to God we agreed together for Deena's healing. As Nina prayed on the phone, with my other hand I reached up in the Spirit and touched the hem of Christ's robe for a friend that I loved and adored. In that very moment the Holy Spirit turned around and said to me, “And that which you ask for your friend, you seek for yourself.” There it was. The truth was out.

I did want healing for my own ailment and I wanted the power of the Holy Spirit to heal others. God told us in His Word that we are to heal the sick, raise the dead, cast out demons. Where was that kind of power and authority in me? Christ said that we would do greater things than He did when He was on Earth. Well I wanted that for me and for Deena! I was undone, crying, praying, an absolute mess. An hour later, drenched in sweat and tears (and I am not certain all of them were mine), I came bursting out of my daughter’s bedroom like it was a telephone booth, knowing I had supernatural powers! In that hour I was transformed, forever different.

All the while Nina was praying I had been agreeing with her and miraculously had begun making a clicking sound with my tongue. What WAS that? I had absolutely NO idea! Shaking and trembling I made my way over to the couch where my husband was watching the news. Boy did I have a newsflash for him. He could tell just by the look of me. My hair was wrecked and my eyes were swollen from weeping. He sat up and looked at me in shock. “Baby, what happened?” I described my experience to him in vivid detail. Crying and shaking, all the while still making these intermittent clicking noises. He looked at me in awe and disbelief. “Kalina, nothing like that has ever happened to me.” “Jeff!” I said. “Nothing like that has ever happened to me either!”

> They looked at me as if I were from another planet

Over the next five days, it was as though I was living in two different worlds: the one everyone else could see and the one the Lord was revealing to me personally. It was surreal, a world within a world. Things were taking place that only I could see and understand. Eyes wide open I tried sharing my experiences with others and they looked at me as if I were from another planet. And that is how I felt. I was on fire! Anyone who has ever been there before knows what this feels like.

On Sunday in the courtyard of church, I was visiting with a group of women telling them about my most amazing encounter with God. I said, "I hope I can remember every single promise that the Holy Spirit spoke over me." A woman said, "Well let's just ask God to seal it in!" They all laid their hands upon me and prayed a simple prayer of faith. I fell to my knees unable to walk or talk. Anyone that knows me agrees that in itself was a miracle. It was peaceful and thrilling all at once. What a journey I was on. Remember the woman from the Bible study who had diagnosed my condition? We met the following day for prayer counseling and right there in her living room she led me through a profound spiritual healing.

This would be the beginning of a gift The Lord was birthing in me. In the weeks that followed I was consumed with prayer and eating the Word of God, drinking in His Spirit like a thirsty camel! I could hear His voice in so many ways. The Holy Spirit was speaking to me non-stop; in the car while driving, by the beach walking the dog, always in the shower. No matter where I went He was there!

One morning I was given a vision of a unique place, a room and time set aside where people could come and receive the same kind of prayer and healing that I had been blessed with. For really the first time in my life I took a bold step of faith moving in a direction foreign to me. Hearing the voice of the Holy Spirit so loud and clear, all I could do was obey. No longer a sleeping princess, He has taught me ever so many things over this past year. From this anointed adventure a Prayer Room was born. What a blessing it was when one of the first people to come in was my friend Deena. Today Deena has experienced a tremendous amount of healing. We are standing together in prayer trusting God for those things which we do not yet see.

THE WAY

Awake, Oh Sleeper (Ephesians 5:14) Secrets of the Kingdom (Matt 13:11-17)

Speaking in Tongues/Laying on of Hands (Mark 16:17-18) An Alien (Psalm 69:8)

No Matter Where I Go! (Psalm 139:7)

THE DIVINE APPOINTMENT PRAYER ROOM

Heritage Christian Fellowship

190 Avenida La Pata

San Clemente, CA 92672

949.361.1022

www.hcfsc.org

[click on ministries, then prayer]

Standing Stone

Testify

The Spirit himself testifies with our spirit that we are God's children.
Romans 8:16 NIV

Keeping the testimony alive is our responsibility and we can't expect others to do it for us. The testimonies of God should be in our daily conversation. When we review the testimonies and meditate on them, we remember the great and marvelous works of the Lord, renewing our minds and training ourselves to think from the realm of faith.

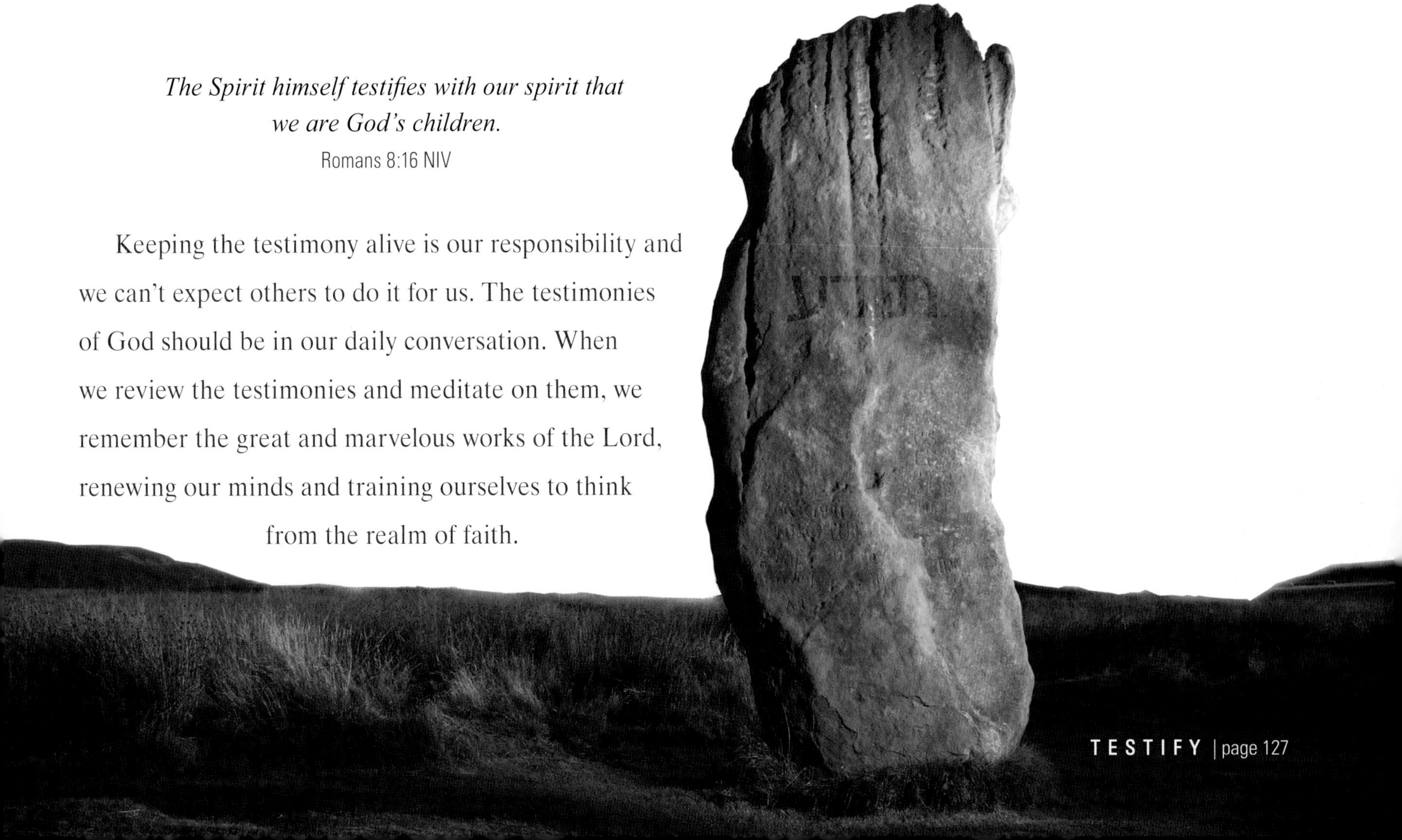

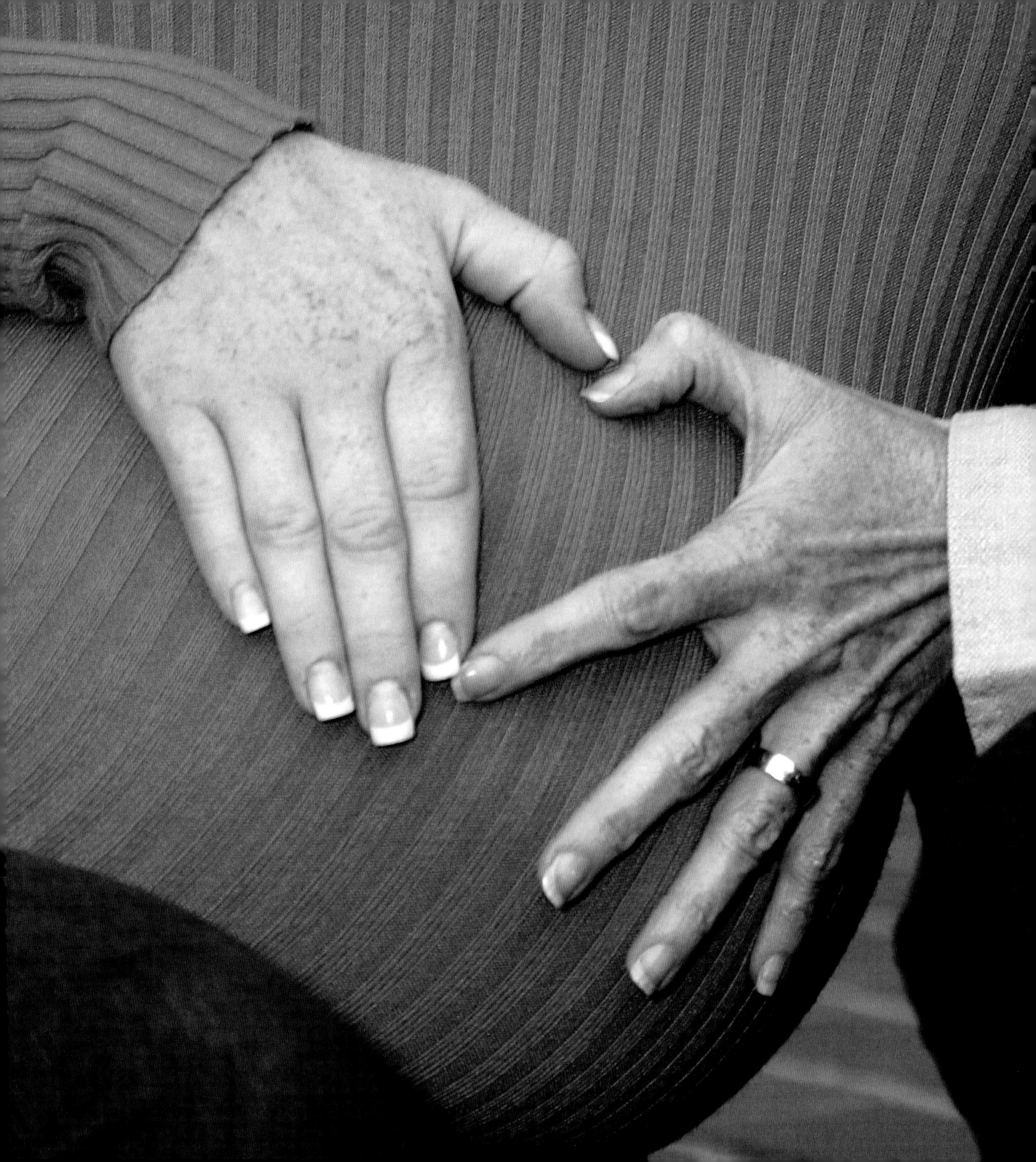

Life or Death?

KoKo

Remember that we have no more faith at any time than we have in the hour of trial. All that will not bear to be tested is mere carnal competence; fair-weather faith is no faith.

C.H. Spurgeon

Bright Lights

When we first saw KoKo it was on a stage. She came out in bright lights before a crowded audience. They would applaud her even more after hearing her speak; in fact, after she delivered her testimony there would not be a dry eye in the house. We were having dinner at a fundraiser for the Pregnancy Resource Center. KoKo was a dynamic and engaging speaker, incredibly vibrant, beautiful and composed. She was a young twenty something with big eyes that reflected wonder at what she was about to share, perhaps because she knew it was by the very hand of God that she was standing there and telling us her story. I confess that we were taken off guard because KoKo did not appear to be pregnant. We were moved by what she shared that night and wanted to know more. Over the next few months we would spend time interviewing KoKo and hear the rest of her story.

She grew up as a believer with loving parents in a Christian home, even went to a Christian college. Her parents did not just talk about their faith; they walked it out, right in front of her. For many years the family opened their home and their hearts to provide a loving environment for a number of foster kids, seeing each one as a child of God. Back then, her relationship with God was everything.

Giving her testimony KoKo began to describe a series of events that take place in the lives of many young people. She had been living on her own and making choices that would deeply affect her life. Thinking she knew it all she made decisions that would lead her into a string of unhealthy relationships with people who were not the best influences.

The First Kiss

The first time you kiss a boy it feels so amazing, so special. And after that it just begins to feel normal. It seemed that way with sex, too. At first you can't even comprehend it. The idea of having sex sounded like a weird thing to do. And then, after the first time you get used to it and, besides, … everyone else is doing it. It made more sense to have one steady boyfriend rather than always meeting someone new and hooking up with different guys. It was like…well, it's okay because we love each other.

I was dating a boy in college that said he wanted to be in full-time ministry and we became sexually active. I felt like this was a relationship I could trust. Then he ended up sleeping with my girlfriend and marrying her instead. After this rejection I bounced back into the arms of another Christian guy. With a Christian boyfriend it was easy to rationalize having sex if I believed we would

eventually get married. I thought to myself, "Was there any difference being involved with Christian guys or non-Christian guys?" Everyone was sexually active.

Where Does This Go?

Fast forward a few years. KoKo was now dating a young man and working in a high-paced environment for a successful real estate company. Between work and boyfriend, this lifestyle consumed all of her time, thoughts and energy. He showered her with love and attention. They had good times doing fun and exciting things. Every weekend was a party as he lavished gifts and attention on her. He made her feel special. On the outside everything seemed glamorous, but on the inside she began to struggle.

KoKo was worried and felt anxious. Something was happening to her physically that was affecting her emotions. She began to have doubts and concerns about her future. Based on her past she wondered, "Where will this relationship go?" knowing she had missed her period.

A Year of Change

"January 2009 I said this is going to be my year! And on January 6th I found out I was pregnant." I said, "Oh wow! New Year's Resolution? This is not what I was planning! My immediate thought was to make this disappear."

Her mind raced as she tried to figure out what to do. At this point she believed keeping things a secret was best.

"I knew my family would be super supportive, but I didn't want to disappoint them." I did not want my friends to find out that I was pregnant, and with no ring on my finger." This was hard enough for her to deal with; she could not imagine how things would be if this situation were brought to light. It was not a good time for a baby. She was young and her relationship with her boyfriend was anything but secure. Hoping that things would go away with a simple phone call, she made an appointment for an abortion and waited anxiously as the date was set for weeks away.

The Appointment

"The abortion clinic was booked and, so for two weeks I agonized over my decision, living daily with the secret. It just started to consume me as each day went by it became more of a torment. I'm not sure I can do this. I don't think this is the right answer." The facade of keeping it all together broke over lunch with friends when KoKo discovered that everyone at work knew she was pregnant. At that moment, knowing she could not walk through this alone, she decided to call her parents. The scripture tells us that if we train up a child in the way that they should go, when they are old they will not depart from it. Proverbs 22:6

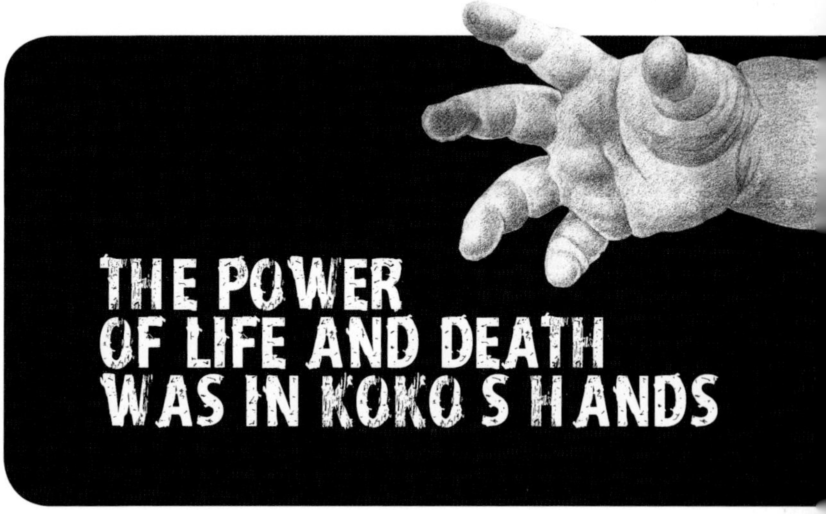

"I phoned my family in tears and my dad came and picked me up. At home, we talked about my circumstances. My mom remembered hearing about the Pregnancy Resource Center at church, just the Sunday before. My little sister brought home a baby bottle that had the PRC info inside. It was to be used to collect coins for donation to the Center." It would prove to be more than just a message in a bottle. KoKo's mother, Susie, wasted no time making the call. Her thoughts were racing as she wondered what KoKo would do. She prayed that they would be able to give KoKo some wise counsel. It was about 3:45 in the afternoon and the Center closed at 4:00.

The Divine Appointment

The founder, Jane Wahl, just happened to be the very person answering the phone that day. "Is there any way we can come in right now and talk to someone?" KoKo's mom asked her. Jane must

have heard the desperation in her voice because, although the office was closing for the day, she decided to stay open and took the appointment immediately.

They sat in the office as KoKo told Jane the whole story. Jane listened with compassion and gently informed KoKo that only two choices had to be considered today! Give the baby life, or not. The power of life and death was in KoKo's hands. Would she keep her appointment for the abortion or not?

The Choice

It was the very thought that had been all-consuming to KoKo. Many tears were shed and her heart was broken as she realized that the time scheduled for the abortion was just days away. No matter how much she had wanted this problem to disappear, she knew the difference between right and wrong. Between all her tears she could finally see the truth clearly for the very first time.

"At that moment I perceived that God had a much bigger and better plan for me and my baby." God tells us in His Word that He has plans for hope and a future, and this option of abortion would not be in my future. It was a miracle that the life of this child was saved only three days away from death.

Today is a new day and a different picture emerges. All things have become new. The baby, a beautiful little daughter with red hair like her mother's and her grandmother's, was born on September 7th at 5:15 in the morning. KoKo is proud of the decision she made to give life.

Filled with joy she holds her newborn baby in her arms and gazes lovingly upon the small child's face. "She is the apple of my eye and I love her so much."

It is not easy being a single mom and raising the baby without a dad in the home. Like any good parent I want to give my daughter every advantage in life. She deserves to be raised in the same kind of loving home that was given to me.

Learning to walk by faith and not by sight, KoKo has said to God, "Okay, Lord, I'm ready to face whatever you have for me and I am grateful for the love and support of my family.

Therefore, prepare your minds for action; be self controlled;
set your hope fully on grace to be given you when Jesus Christ is revealed.
As obedient children, do not conform to the evil desires you had when you lived in ignorance,
but just as he who called you is holy, be holy because I am holy.
1 Peter 1:13-16 NIV

Under Construction

Pat and Deb

At first Pat and Deb didn't know exactly what hit them. Sure, they had been through these construction cycles before as small business owners, but the California real estate market had always proved strong and this would be just another bump in the road. For over twenty-five years they had worked hard together building a successful design business, wallpapering model homes in Orange County. They hadn't had a paycheck in over a year; their savings account was empty and credit card debt mounted as they tried to keep the wolves at bay. If they didn't sell their home soon, foreclosure was certain.

Who wouldn't be overwhelmed with their current situation? Pat and Deb were weary of the ups and downs of the business in addition to the grind of seven-day weeks just to keep their heads above water. They hoped this road they were on would bring the golden egg of success, living by the motto "God helps those who help themselves." Now this one area they held on to so tight was being chopped away.

The couple had accepted Jesus Christ as their Lord and Savior in 1979. However, although they professed their love for Him, over the years He got crowded out. Remember, they were too busy with the business of this world. The truth was they had abandoned their First Love. Their hearts felt as bankrupt as their savings accounts. They had nothing left.

Where the Rubber Meets the Road

The Lord would not allow this to continue, as He loved them too much. It was time for godly discipline to enter their lives. Through this new journey of spiritual correction their relationship with God and each other would grow stronger and closer. As Pat called out to God, the Lord gave him a word: "You shall be holy for I am Holy." Pat began to ponder this with the Lord and understand its profound relevance as the world he knew was falling apart.

Their external circumstances were powering their desire for a closer relationship with God. Now that He had their undivided attention, God revealed to Pat and Deb His desire for an intimate relationship. They were encouraged to keep their eyes on Him, release control and finally rest in Him.

Trust in the Lord with all of your heart and lean not on your own understanding; in all of your ways acknowledge him, and he will make your paths straight.
Proverbs 3:5-6 NIV

The Lord had allowed this trial to head them into a right mindset and deeper relationship with Him. As they drew closer to the Lord they could see He was actually rescuing them. They began daily to humble themselves and surrender everything, giving Him praise and thanksgiving for their situation. They started each day reading the Bible and spending quality time with Him. They took every day as it came, not knowing the outcome but now trusting in God. He was now the Master builder of their lives, and they were under major construction.

Being in their fifties, they had to redefine who they were in a new job market. They began to pray about direction and the Lord opened doors for them to walk though providing work for food and basic needs. Their million-dollar home they had purchased several years before to house their business and provide retirement was now a ball and chain around their necks.

Many things entered their minds concerning this home. Will the Lord allow them to keep it, or are they going to have to let it foreclose? Will it be a short sale, or do they file for bankruptcy? Where would they move and who would rent to them? All the questions were mind-boggling and were surrendered in prayer. They made a decision to trust God and He would provide for them. What a difference! This way of living was so new to them.

Like many others, Pat and Deb were caught up in the nation's souring economy, the downturn of the California real estate market and decisions they had made. At this point their faith was being built up and God, Who makes no mistakes, knew in advance that they would go through this crisis. They stood on the following scripture:

And we know that in all things God works for the good of those who love him,
who have been called according to his purpose.
Romans 8:28 NIV

How glorious it was to see God answer their prayers and move in such miraculous ways, above and beyond what they could even imagine.

No, they didn't win the lottery, but they began to see how their circumstances, which were so overwhelming to them, were changing one by one, little by little, and in such a supernatural way. They were headed for a big remodel.

After much prayer and discussion, Pat and Deb decided to short sell their home. It was getting closer and closer to the foreclosure date and after one potential buyer had fallen out they anxiously waited to see what was going to happen. One morning a young couple came to look at the house and decided it was a perfect match. Not only did they want to buy the house that day, they offered all cash and the bank accepted it. Weeks later, Pat and Deb received a letter from the bank saying the debt had been forgiven. The slate had been wiped clean, just as God had forgiven them. This was one of many miracles.

During this whirlwind of change, their beloved dog, Amigo, was diagnosed with cancer. They didn't have the money to even consider the surgery that might provide hope for their precious pet. Amigo was like the child they never had. Through a series of events they were put in touch with a veterinarian who not only took on the case but also paid in full all the medical cost of this expensive procedure. This was someone Pat and Deb had never met before. Another miracle.

With the sale of their home, they had to find somewhere to move, and quickly. Barely having enough money to scrape together for the first and last month's rent, they began to look at rentals. Who would rent to us? Shocked by the high cost of renting they pressed forward in faith and found something on Craigslist that might work for them. After setting up an appointment to view the property they met with the owners, a wonderful Christian couple. Pat and Deb began to tell their story, being very candid about their financial situation and how they had lost everything. Having a kindred Spirit, the couple was moved to make it work for everyone. Today they live in this beautiful home that God handpicked for them.

Patrick and Deb are closer today with God and with each other than ever before. They purpose to communicate daily with the Lord and one another, sharing what He is doing in their hearts and lives. "When one of us is down, we both just stop and pray!"

They don't know what the future holds, but they know who holds the future. Last month, after writing their testimony, the Lord provided all the money they needed to pay bills for the first time in two years without a deficit. They are seeking and trusting Him for next month.

"We testify here today that we are better people as a result of taking this journey on the higher road with God. We believe and trust in His grace and provision more than ever before. His ways are not our ways."

"In conclusion, we want to share this humorous side note with you. We read a story about Billy Graham and his wife. As they were driving they noticed a sign by the side of the road. Ruth Graham said she would like this quote put on her tombstone — and so would Patrick and I:"

END OF CONSTRUCTION

THANK YOU FOR YOUR PATIENCE

Life is Unpredictable

Vel

WOULD MY FAITH OUTLAST THE TRIALS I FACED OVER THE YEARS? I KNEW GOD HAD A DESTINY FOR ME, AND I WANTED TO FINISH THE RACE...AND FINISH WELL. THIS IS MY TESTIMONY.

Imagine that you are married with children, a working professional, educated and successful. You come home from work with your nine-year-old daughter in hand only to discover that every single item has been removed from your home. Not even a mattress or pillow for your children to sleep on. Everything packed up and vanished. No word, no warning. Even the bank account has been cleaned out...robbed of everything.

<September 8, 2005>

Vel became a single mother, without a penny to her name or a change of clothing for her kids. Recovering from the shock, she tried to gather her wits as she made plans to get a small loan. She went to a local thrift store to buy an outfit for each of her children and a bed to sleep on.

Struggling from the abandonment of her husband and all the chaos surrounding it, she didn't take much notice of the bleeding that was occurring. At that point she thought it was perhaps her monthly cycle, but the bleeding persisted. She attributed this to the stress and anxiety she was experiencing, deeply worried for her children. She made an appointment to see a doctor who performed an ultrasound. The doctor saw something wrong in her ovaries and uterus. Surgery was mandatory.

< September 26, 2005>

Vel had a complete hysterectomy. Ten hours after surgery she began to crash; the doctors did not know what was happening. Her blood pressure dropped rapidly; her stomach was bloated and she could not breathe. Vel was rushed back into the operating room. Before going under she was asked, "Is there anybody you want to contact right now? You might not make it."

Her mind was racing. She did not know where to turn or what to do. All of her family lived in the Philippines. She gave them Kelle's name, a girlfriend who lived nearby. They wheeled her into the O.R. for a second round of surgery. Turned out there was internal bleeding from the hysterectomy, which explained the low blood pressure and why she was crashing. Days later when she was stable, doctors released Vel and she was able to go home, if you could call it that. The kids were staying with friends, so she was by herself in an empty house.

For a while everything seemed okay until she started to develop a fever. Kelle determined to check on her from time to time throughout the day. Finding her delirious with a fever of 105 she shouted, "Vel! Vel! Wake up! Wake up! Kelle placed her hand upon Vel's shoulder to shake her to consciousness. She was terrified as she felt the fire burning in Vel's body. Immediately she called the doctor and they were advised to go to the E.R. Vel was readmitted once again.

Over the course of many days she would travel back and forth to the hospital consulting with numerous specialists, but nothing they said prepared her for the news yet to come.

<September 30, 2005>

Stage Four Uterine Cancer. Chemo and radiation were recommended. They referred her to an oncologist, which began a journey of treatment that would span the next three years! Needless to say, she was overwhelmed and ready for the month of September to end.

<2005-2008> Learning Humility

Over time, the realization of her cancer settled in. She knew that she was not going to be able to work and would have to go on disability. What would happen to her kids? Pastor Mike encouraged her saying God is with you and He will take care of everything for you. Don't worry. Keep looking up and everything will be okay. She had only met this pastor a few weeks before her first surgery. Little did she know that this church would become her family and over time would teach her how to receive.

People would say to her, Vel, you need help and we are here for you. Pastor Mike wanted her to know they would provide for her family. "I don't know why I had such a hard time receiving help, perhaps because my parents had taught me to be self-sufficient. They instilled a 'you can do it yourself' attitude and yet I realized I could not do this alone. There came a point when I had to lay down my pride, let go of myself."

The church rallied around Vel, wanting to demonstrate the love of Christ in practical ways. They gave her money, paid her rent, brought in meals and took care of her and the children. People were serving in every way they could. The Lord was providing for all her needs through her new church family. They truly loved and cared for her.

<March 2006>

Stage Two Bone Cancer. Vel was to experience three intense years of chemo treatment. Only six months into the process they also diagnosed her with Osteosarcoma: Stage two bone cancer. Doctors found the cancer in her elbow and performed surgery to remove it. During these difficult times, her faith was made stronger.

"I hung on to His promise all the while, considering my prayers already answered. It is done! God says whatever it is you pray for, it is completed. My faith ensures that this will happen. When I prayed for healing, it wasn't only for my physical illness. I needed emotional healing for my broken heart and the loss of my marriage."

"Have faith in God," Jesus answered. "I tell you the truth, if anyone says to this mountain, 'Go, throw yourself into the sea,' and does not doubt in his heart but believes that what he says will happen, it will be done for him. Therefore I tell you, whatever you ask for in prayer, believe that you have received it, and it will be yours. And when you stand praying, if you hold anything against anyone, forgive him, so that your Father in heaven may forgive you your sins."

Mark 11:22 NIV

<October 23, 2007> The Blessing and the Healing

Vel had heard about a healing ministry at Bethel Church in Redding, California. Unfortunately she had no money and absolutely no idea how to get there. Her best friend from Chicago called and asked what she wanted for her birthday. HEALING! Vel said. Her friend suggested the possibility of going for healing at Bethel Church. "I told her I could be healed anywhere, here or Redding." She said, you're going! I'm sending plane tickets for you and your daughter right now, paid in full.

Before leaving on the plane to Redding, Vel noticed her arm was still black and blue from her recent surgery. Many friends dropped by to pray and bless them with extra money. Praise God! He knew in advance the exact amount that they would need. Every detail was taken care of.

"Selah and I left for The Open Heaven Conference at Bethel Church, where God would meet us and I would receive a complete healing in my elbow. The manifestation of healing was so evident; as I looked at my arm I noticed there was no trace of bruising and mobility was restored. All the way home I felt love from the Father and was ministered to."

"I know God is so very good. Over the years He has allowed my circumstances to break me. I'm changed into the woman who can run the race and finish well. Through all the pain and struggle, God was trying to show Himself to me. I had to surrender and say, 'Okay, God, okay. I understand that in receiving there is blessing for those who give.' Because of these trials, I have learned to be content in everything."

"I know what it is to be in need, and I know what it is to have plenty. I have learned the secret of being content in any and every situation, whether well fed or hungry, whether living in plenty or in want."
Philippians 4:12 NIV

"The Lord showed me His great love through the body of Christ. He used this experience to connect me with people whom I would not ordinarily meet. He showered His love upon me so that I could do the same for others. It is through my faith and the love from the church that I know I am not alone. He is always by my side as I run the race set before me and fulfill my destiny."

<Feb 2009>

Vel Perfect Health Party - Friends celebrate with Vel in her victory over cancer.

Naomi

June

My son got a new job far from his home. When it got old driving back and forth every day, I invited him, his new wife and her children to move in to my home. When they married, I prayed that the Lord would give her and I a special relationship, one much like Ruth and Naomi of the Bible (book of Ruth). Needless to say, it was not easy for a new wife to move in to her mother-in-law's home. We didn't know each other well, but we both committed to make our new living arrangement work.

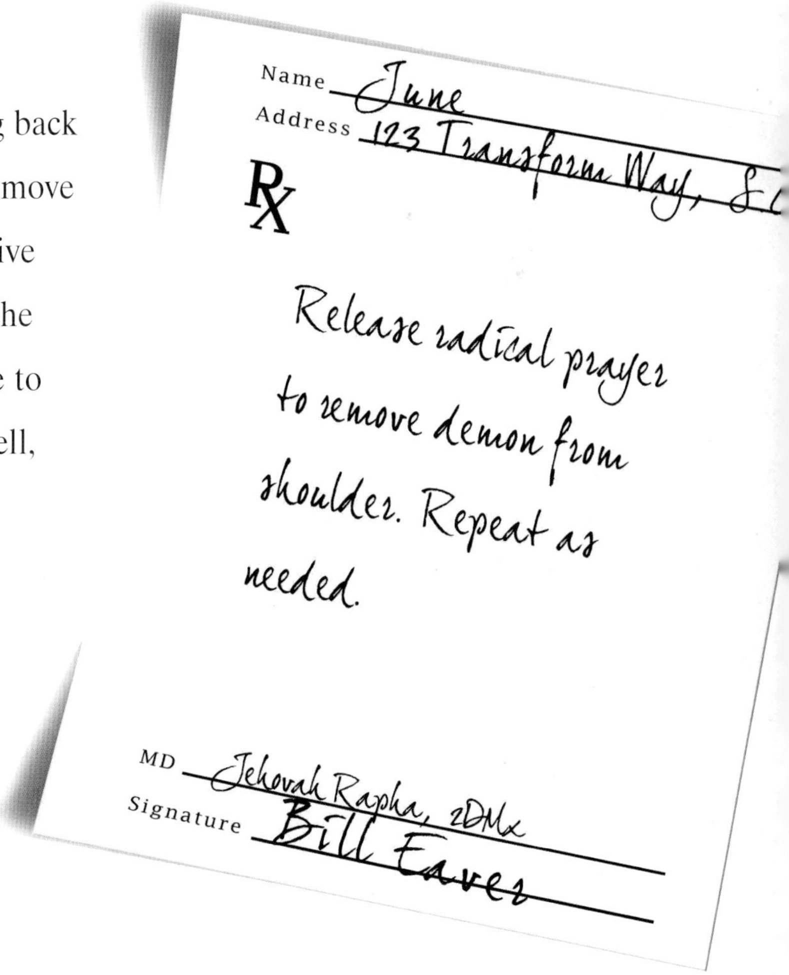

Shortly after they moved in, I had an appointment with my doctor, who is a Christian. In the course of our conversation, he told me in a matter of fact way that I had a demon on my shoulder. He asked me what I wanted him to do? I said, "Pray!" After he prayed he said, "It's still there."

I wanted this spirit off of me! I immediately began to pray, standing firm and resisting the devil. I clenched my fists, saying, "I don't know what your name is, but I take authority over you in the name of Jesus Christ and command you to leave in no uncertain terms." The Bible says Jesus spoke sternly to the demons and so did I! The doctor said, "O my goodness, it's gone!"

All the way home I kept asking the Lord, "What was that all about?" By the time I entered my living room, I realized what that demon was. It was a spirit of criticism that I had about my daughter-in-law. Being a young mom with small children, she had quite a different standard of housekeeping than I did. I never verbalized my critical thoughts, but they were constantly eating at my mind.

Realizing what had transpired, I repented to the Lord for being so critical. I committed to change my thinking and live in this house with a good attitude showing kindness, joy, and helping wherever I could. I thanked the Lord for setting me free. That very day I experienced a wonderful peace all over my home.

Some time later I was in bed asleep when my daughter-in-law knocked on my door. She had been to a Bible study that evening. She said the Lord revealed to her that the trouble we were having was because of her bad attitude. She was sorry. With forgiveness in my heart, I described to her how I had prayed that the Lord would give us a relationship like Ruth and Naomi: warm, loving, and filled with mutual respect for one another.

Ten years later, my son and his wife went to Israel with the church. He had not had a paycheck in months, so they traveled on a shoestring budget with no extra money. To my surprise, my daughter-in-law brought me a gift from Israel. It was just a small package. When I opened it, there was a pair of silver dangling earrings inscribed with a Hebrew name. She asked me if I knew what it meant. I had no idea. My daughter-in-law's face was radiant with love as she said, "Naomi."

With tears in my eyes I hugged her, for this precious gift she so lovingly gave me was an answer to my prayer so many years before. My precious Lord never ceases to amaze me with His tender ways and unspeakable love. To Him be all glory, honor, and praise for now and all eternity.

Standing Stone

Testify

"For the testimony of Jesus is the spirit of prophecy."
Revelation 19:10c NIV

The prophetic anointing does not just declare what God wants to do, but also carries creative power to bring what is declared into being. Every time a testimony is shared it releases the spirit of prophesy ...if God can do it for me, He can do it for you!

AMAZING THINGS

Photo courtesy of Mike Takaki

happen

Being able to capture the very moment in a photograph is one of my greatest passions.

All The TIME

Evidence of Things Unseen

Jeffrey

Amazing things happen around us all the time, and being able to see them is natural. Being able to capture the very moment in a photograph is something that has been one of my greatest passions. I look for timing in life as images that, when captured, have the power to move and inspire. Being a professional photographer and a committed surfer, everything I do is from the perspective of looking at the world through the eye of a camera lens or the eye of a wave. That was my point of view.

But now my perspective has changed. I am no longer the same. God has given me a supernatural vision! Once struck by blindness I am now able to see the miracles of the Father's love in a way that leaves me on fire for Christ and filled with the power of the Holy Spirit.

Several years ago a radical life-changing event would start out like the common flu.

The difference was it never left, persisting with a dangerously high fever for days, which turned into weeks. Going to the doctor every other day became visits to a variety of specialists instead. And still no answers. All the while my body was shutting down. It was hard getting through one day at a time, let alone thinking about the future. Feeling like I was having heart attacks and spending midnight hours at the ER, this routine was beginning to have a slow-burning impact on my family, my business and my sanity.

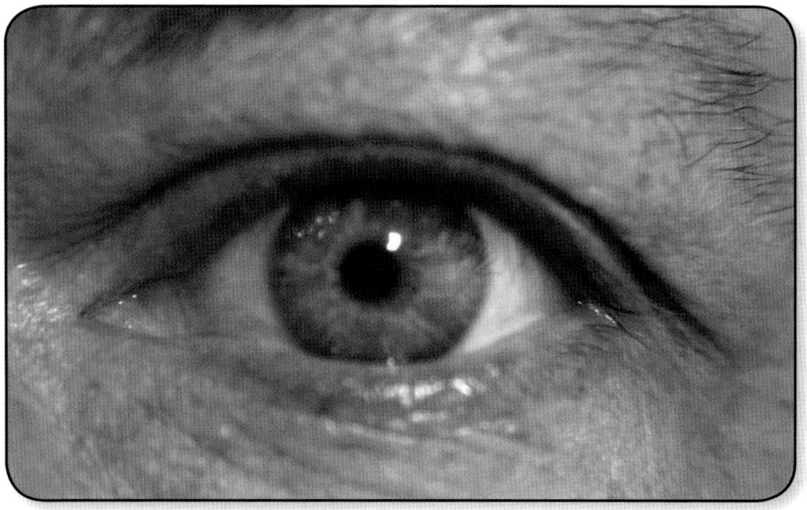

Walking down the hallway of the hospital one day, a bolt of confusion and panic shot through me as the vision in my left eye suddenly disappeared, off like a light switch! Instantly there was a huge blind spot in my eye. It wasn't light or dark; it was just void. Imagine you see a picture and suddenly a big piece of it is simply missing. Already in the hospital, no one could explain what had just happened to me. I found myself paralyzed with anxiety.

What a nightmare! More specialists would be required to try to solve my awful dilemma. The diagnosis was ranging from optic neuritis to the possibility of advanced multiple sclerosis. Gotta love doctors for their sacrifice to heal others, but remember they too are only human. During that time I went to a total of eight neuro-ophthalmologists and neurologists and was told the same depressing news.

GET YOUR AFFAIRS IN ORDER

At best, the doctors said I had a few months to live. One specialist said, "Get your affairs in order," as he did not believe that treatment would really help at this point. Easy for you to say, I thought, getting angry. I am too young for this to happen! My heart was broken for my family. It was already emotionally devastating watching our kids go off to school while I lay wasting away on the couch. Now the doctor tells me it's over, I'm done! My wife began to weep helplessly. At that moment it was God's grace that kept me from reacting with a brutal punch to his face. I knew there had to be a better way to fight for my life other than to give the doctor a thrashing for his lack of hope and bedside manner.

Mad with a fire inside that turned into a righteous steam, I was focused on a new direction. It was time to get serious with God, up close and personal. My life depended on it. I was riding a wave of emotion, falling to my knees, begging God for insight in an area that had been crowded by darkness and confusion. What kind of future was there for us without my eyesight? It is what I do! Talk about walking by faith and not by sight!

Reluctantly we scheduled an appointment for massive steroid treatments. It was a few days away and I did not have any peace about it. I'd received eleven different opinions and even though the professionals agreed with each other, something within me disagreed with all of them, vehemently! God was going to show me another way. Even the paperwork of getting another opinion seemed inconceivable, yet He always makes a way when everyone else tells you it is impossible.

By His Spirit, He led me to search out all the information needed to obtain the leading neuro-opthalmologist at the Shiley Eye Center. The office informed me that it would be a 6-month wait just to get an appointment. I did not have the luxury of time.

Yet, God's timing is perfect. I prayed and I pushed. Someone once said that the word push is great an acronym for Pray Until Something Happens. Oh, I prayed all right! God gave me the strength and determination to persevere as I pushed my way into the doctor's office. I faxed the doctor my medial records and, after looking them over, she set up an appointment for the very next morning. In my spirit I knew this appointment would be life saving. There is no other word for it but "a miracle." When God wants a door opened, it opens! A thorough medical history was taken and the doctors confirmed within minutes of their own examination that I did not have optic neuritis and was not going to die from this condition! What?

After hearing so many opinions about how my life would end in this cruel twist of fate, I was blown away by what they just said. I knew it! Not optic neuritis or MS. When the doctors properly diagnosed me they would discover that I had a rare airborne form of Cat Scratch Syndrome called Bartonella Hensla (probably from a feral kitten or a wild cat, when shooting pictures on location in the mountains). The truth I had searched for was finally revealed by God, hidden just for me, not from me. All this time as my faith was being tested and stretched, here was the defining moment in truth that would set me free.

I was assured that my sight would not worsen and that my brain would compensate for the partial loss, possibly even heal by itself over time. And some of it has! Praise God because of that I have been able to live my life: surfing, taking pictures. More importantly, I am grateful every day when I see my beautiful family and how God has blessed us.

My eyesight is a gift that I do not take for granted. And with a newfound vision for miracles, God has given me opportunity to minister to others through the power of prayer. Getting to know Him so closely throughout this ordeal has given me a heart of compassion and understanding for what others need in times of trial and tribulation.

Let me put it to you this way, when a person needs a miracle, **there is nothing like getting prayer from someone who knows that miracles are possible** because they have seen it happen with their own eyes!

Wow. He is so amazing. I love God so much. I never thought that I could love anyone more than my wife and kids. Dude, I am a thrill seeker and an adrenaline junkie, and I am here to tell you there is nothing more electric than living in the Spirit, walking by faith and not by sight! Nothing is more powerful than knowing that you are loved by the God of the universe and that He has a perfect plan for you. You are created in His image and given a Spirit of love, power and a sound mind.

Electric Livi

After serving on the prayer team for some time I experience miracles on a daily basis as I walk from glory to glory in the Spirit of the Almighty God.

Story #1

Loving the solitude of surf I went out one day determined to take as many waves as possible. Some days you really want to be out there alone. No one was in the water and I positioned myself to get a good workout. After a few waves, a lone guy paddles out and sits as close as possible, in my personal space. I thought, Dude, you've got the whole beach to surf, do you really need to sit right next to me? (Hey, I'm human.) At that moment God gave me a command: "Go tell that guy I love him." What, God? I don't wanna do that. I'm tired and I've had a rough people day. I hear the voice again. Okay already. Dying to my own selfish desires, I say to the guy in a casual voice, Hey, man, Jesus loves you. "What did you say?" he asked. Louder, I repeat myself. I just wanted to let you know that Jesus loves you. Whoa! That opened up a conversation almost without end. The guy poured out his heart and shared how his two children had been healed recently and he knew it was a miracle. As the two of us sat in the water and talked, God gave revelation to some of his needs. We began praying together until it was done. What an incredible time in the Spirit! Paddling in I realized I hadn't caught more than three waves. God had better plans for me. Goes to show that God, who sees all and knows all, can send someone, anyone, to pray for you. Heal you. Deliver you. Right where you are.

Story #2

One evening, a spirit of depression moved over me that I could not seem to shake. It was beyond troubling and serious. Everyone I knew to pray with was unavailable and I felt like this was a crossroads kind of moment. Being frustrated, I actually was entertaining thoughts of giving up in certain areas of my life where breakthrough was taking too long. As I went to bed I prayed:

My God, my God, why have you forsaken me?
Why are you so far from saving me,
so far from the words of my groaning?
O my God, I cry out by day, but you do not answer,
by night, and am not silent.

Psalm 22:1,2 NIV

weeping may remain for a night but rejoicing comes in the morning.

Psalm 30:5b NIV

And so this day I would experience a Divine Appointment house call. God would send an angel in the form of a cable guy to pray the most anointed prayer over me! He walked into one of the bedrooms and stepped right back out and said, "Hey, you are a believer and I am supposed pray for you!" Right there this gnarly prayer warrior had a word of knowledge for me; it was unreal. I was moved and ministered to right in my own home! This cable guy was speaking in tongues and casting off every spirit of depression and the like. He anointed our house with oil and blessed everyone in it! Hallelujah!

Right after that I had an appointment at the church. Pastor Mike came out of his office and said, "Hey, I was just looking for you. Can you come to the hospital and pray for a man in a coma? He had a heart attack and is on life support. His wife is really shaken up and wants us to pray for him as soon as we can get there. The doctors told her to consider pulling the plug. It's pretty serious."

Apparently God wanted me back in active service for His glory. Thankfully the cable guy had just prayed me up to full and overflowing. I was ready! We get to the hospital to see the woman and she is clinging to hope for her husband. Mike and I prayed for the two of them, laying hands on her husband. We declared God's promises with power and authority, the way that Christ commissioned us to do! Before leaving, we knew the man was healed! The next day he was walking around without any side effects from the heart attack or the coma! Praise God. It was a miracle.

Our True Inheritance

Joe and Ladeshia

Joe's story

I grew up in a very religious family...I say that almost with a cringe. My grandparents were strict and they passed it on to my dad. Going to church was mandatory. We were spiritually legalistic and without love. My dad was a great provider of material things; unfortunately he wasn't able to demonstrate any physical or emotional affection.

The environment in our home was pretty unhappy and controlled by my overbearing father. I would like to think my dad meant well. Unfortunately, he had many shortcomings from his own childhood that came out in the way he raised us. I remember as kids hearing Dad's truck drive up and cringing; we would run for cover. We were afraid of Dad and didn't want to be around him. Mom tried to overcompensate for his lack, but the truth was, she wasn't able to protect us from him. My childhood began in fear.

Ladeshia's story

I was raised on an Evangelical Christian commune. It was all or nothing. You were in it 110 percent. My three younger brothers and I remember having nightly meetings in our home and our parents would spend hours just worshiping the Lord. Often we would go with them to different venues. We couldn't wait to watch them sing. Everything we did growing up as young children was completely centered on Christ. I was fortunate to be raised in a home with such a loving family.

JOE

Ladeshia and I were raised so differently. I grew up in Newport Beach, went to school at USC, locking into the whole atmosphere of success, the trap of affluence and materialism. "What do you drive? Where do you live? Where do you vacation?"

I began pursuing the American Dream, working 80-100 hours a week. I was chasing the dollar and battling day after day. I kept thinking I needed to build a foundation for a career so that I could have it all. I could not see beyond it and continually said, "I am late for an appointment." "I have to go to work." "I am stressed out!" Because of these choices, I failed in my first marriage.

Here I was now in my second marriage with Ladeshia, and it was already suffering from the same symptoms. I was an emotionally unavailable husband. Mentally I was always at work. When I think back, I must have had some qualities that Ladeshia appreciated, otherwise we wouldn't have gotten together.

LADESHIA

Joe and I were both in Cabo and met on a party trip. That is what we had in common. Most of my teenage years had been spent moving away from the Lord, one step at a time. When I met Joe I was not the Christian girl my parents had raised me to be. My life had been about partying with a bunch of girls that were as lost as I was. I heard God's voice, heard His persistent voice, always calling in the background, "Come home to me." Still I wanted to do what I wanted to do. Because of my choices, life was going downhill, one bad relationship after the next.

> If I were to leave, *even temporarily,* **where would I go? I was lost.**

It looked like I was living the good life. Men wanted to be with me because I was pretty. No one ever accused me of not having fun. I didn't spend much time worrying about my actions. If bad things happened, I bounced back quickly, but in my heart, deep down inside, I was miserable. Joe and I were like so many couples that begin a relationship with lots of baggage and fractured pasts. We started off optimistic, full of hope that we would be able to make it. The one thing that held us together was the fact that we genuinely liked each other.

JOE

I felt like I had pretty good intentions. I meant well, but what I did was squash Ladeshia's feelings. I had so much on my plate and just kept adding more. I was driven, unbalanced and lived in denial. I was not available emotionally or physically for my wife and family. I recognized in me this part of my DNA makeup was from my dad and here I was now living it.

LADESHIA

Throughout our marriage, Joe trampled me emotionally and I took it. I didn't have enough inner strength to stand up for myself and acted out in a very passive-aggressive manner, and I was unwilling to face a lot of my own issues and pain from my past. Being stubborn and prideful, I didn't want to let it go. Joe would do things that I knew were clearly not right for our relationship, but I didn't speak up. I realized I didn't have any healthy boundaries and had completely lost my sense of self worth. At this point I didn't know what to do. Should I leave? If I were to leave, even temporarily, where would I go? I was lost.

JOE

I was like a Dr. Jekyll and Mr. Hyde. I would be loving and close one moment but emotionally detached and withdrawn the next. It was a vicious cycle. As soon as Ladeshia became more intimate, I would verbally smack her back. It was very real. I knew I didn't want to be like my dad, but my behavior said otherwise. On my own strength, changing my behavior was impossible.

LADESHIA

I never trusted Joe. We had checked out from one another and there was not much left of the relationship. It's true; I was totally afraid of him.

Even though **I was to blame** *for what happened,* I could not forgive her.

JOE

I did everything I could to push Ladeshia into the affair. I trampled her in every aspect: as a mother, a wife, and even a child of God. This is our true-life story, and we pray others will benefit from our mistakes. Even though I was to blame for what happened, I could not forgive her. Intellectually, I forgave her and moved beyond. But emotionally it was like carrying around a sack of rocks every day. The affair tormented me and I was tired of having this thing spin around in my mind. We went to counseling, read self-help books and talked about it a lot. But, the true forgiveness that only is from God hadn't come yet.

I don't know exactly what happened. But one day I just said, "Lord, I don't want this. Help me. I know you forgave her. PLEASE! Help me to do the same. Take it away!" And He did! He took it as far as the East is from the West. It was gone! I prayed and God lifted it that day like flipping a switch. It happened so quickly. It gave me so much confidence that God was there for me. "Seek and ye shall find." Such a simple truth yet so profound. One moment I was covered in self-loathing, anger and unforgiveness, and the next moment,

"I waited patiently for the Lord; he turned to me and heard my cry. He lifted me out of the slimy pit, out of the mud and mire; he set my feet on the rock and gave me a firm place to stand."
Psalm 40:1-2 NIV

LADESHIA

I was beginning to feel things stirring inside of me. I knew it had to be the hand of the Lord. My mother was encouraging me to turn my life around and invited me to a young moms Bible study. With each step God was doing something new in my life. He was changing me from the inside out. I realized I had been on the fence for many years. I had one foot in my old lifestyle, seemingly glamorous and exciting. Was I really a desperate housewife in Orange County? I began having emotional breakdowns and reached out for prayer. I had even forgotten how to pray for myself. It was really quite foreign because I had been away from God for so long.

It was like starting over. I had to make new friends. I felt very uncomfortable not knowing if the girls in the small group were sincere. One new friend, Amy, was so wonderful, I could hardly believe it! I thought, are you serious? Is this girl even for real? It took me a long time to learn how to develop healthy relationships. What real support and friendship showed me was the love of the Lord. God was healing me of being so focused on Joe's problems.

JOE

Our problems were challenging and I was making them worse. Although I had forgiven Ladeshia and myself for what happened, we still had more adversities to face. We had bought a house at the high end of the market and for the next two years I spent my evenings and weekends doing a remodel, working with my dad. All this and a full time job! No wonder I started to drink. I told myself alcohol was a way to handle the stress.

Soon after, my business came to a halt and so did the paychecks. No income, no savings and all of the credit cards were maxed. Our lives were spinning out of control. In the middle of that we had another baby. Because of the construction, Ladeshia and the kids were living with her parents and I never even saw the family. Everything was collapsing and there was nothing I could do about it. We were losing our home — a home I had spent years working on and we never lived in it when it was completed! I felt like I was losing my sanity. I was drowning in sorrow and alcohol while doing the best I could to keep up a good front. Or was I?

LADESHIA

Living back at home with my parents, I felt safe and experienced a lot of spiritual and personal growth. Yet, there was a part of me that was upset by the fact that Joe was not dealing well with all of our problems. He was on a rapid decline. Our daughters never even saw their dad. He was like a rat on a wheel trying to crack out the huge monthly expenses. Meanwhile, I made a decision to reach out to others and fight the battle spiritually. I began to attend Minka's prayer group where mighty intercessors would pray over my family. These mature women of God fought for Joe's salvation, his spirit and his life.

They fought the good fight using the sword of the Spirit and the Word of God to fight against the powers and principalities of spiritual warfare: alcoholism, false idols of money and greed, strongholds of pride, isolation and self. I felt so fortunate that God worked through so many people to support us and love us throughout this time in our lives.

JOE

Everything was collapsing and there was nothing I could do about it. I watched as all of my dreams came crashing down. The real-estate market was in the tank. Our mortgage was upside down and then I lost my job. I knew that my dream house was getting away from me. We stopped receiving a paycheck at the same time the house payment went to $9,000 per month. Our credit card debt was out of control. Foreclosure was imminent and bankruptcy was around the corner.

We were on this psycho spin and finally, when I got to the end, humbling myself, I went to Ladeshia and said, "I am so sorry." Personally, I was desperate for change. Slowly, I began to rely on the Lord more to develop spiritually. I was so thick-headed. Even after the affair, when God walked me through forgiveness, I still went on my merry way. Now I had to face my demons, get real, and make some changes.

For me, it was critical to become an active participant with the Lord in all aspects of the church and necessary to place myself around other people. No more hibernating!

I began to attend a group healing and recovery meeting that met on a weekly basis. It kept my heart soft as I heard others share their pain and victories. In the beginning I was afraid to go. I didn't want to be hypocritical if I couldn't keep it up. I realized that was one way the enemy tries to keep us bound to our sin. Christ died to set us free, and I needed to walk in that liberty.

In addition to the Bible, I read as many books as I could in an effort to understand what had been happening to me. For the first time, prayer became real and powerful as I spent time talking with my heavenly Father. Desperately wanting to learn more about how to pray, I began a journey of studying what God had to say about it. My eyes began to open and I couldn't get enough. The Holy Spirit had come into my life and breathed into me. I was spiritually dead before and now was receiving daily mouth-to-mouth resuscitation. I felt like both Ladeshia and I finally caught the wave of all the prayers that had gone up for us over the many years. It was incredibly liberating and I will be forever grateful!

LADESHIA

Our home today is very different in so many ways spiritually and physically. To begin with, we all live under one roof together. It is a much happier place to be. When Daddy comes home the girls are holding hands and running around in a circle singing, "Daddy's home, Daddy's home!" Today we know we are called to a higher purpose and have better skills to avoid the blowups. We're doing our best to deal with the issues in a godly manner.

JOE

I still feel so young in Christ, like a kid really, even after all that I have done to learn more and educate myself in the Word. I am grateful for the daily things, the daily bread. Together, Ladeshia and I are so much happier. Individually and together as a family we have a lot of joy and peace today. We turn to others and reach out instead of going into that dark hole that consumed us before, that was merely fear and isolation. Fear is the opposite of faith. It is one of the ways the enemy strategically tries to separate us from the family of believers and from the love of God.

I wake up now saying, "Good morning, God. Come fill me." I want Him to shine on me so that others can see it. I now pray continuously and know that if I am having a dialogue with the Father, I will never be away from Him again. We live in gratitude as we seek the Lord, taking every thought captive. We have an amazing amount of peace, the peace that surpasses all understanding.

LADESHIA

Our circumstances might look bleak to those who cannot see what is happening spiritually. But we have faith and it is strong in the Lord! People say, why aren't you freaking out? You have no job, living month to month in a rental house. Yet the Lord is providing our daily bread and we feel blessed. We are all so grateful. The kids are so excited to have their father back in their lives, just as Joe and I are excited to have our heavenly Father back in ours! We wait in anticipation of our future with the Lord's handprint on it instead of our own.

Prisoner

Scott

"I'm not going to survive this. There's nothing left to live for. I give up!"

Through tears I fashioned a noose from the bed sheet eyeing the light fixture at the top of my jail cell. It should hold me I thought. What was there left to live for? I had failed in every area of my life. The withdrawal from drug addictions would probably kill me anyway. What good was I now? I prepared to end my life. I had become a prisoner of my own making.

Years earlier, around Thanksgiving of 1984, I received a blow that changed my life forever. Living in Maui at the time, I thought I was at the height of health and happiness: surfing, partying and living free. Over the years many of my friends died from drug overdoses; others were facing jail sentences. Somehow escaping both, I was enjoying all the fantasies of a twenty-nine-year-old who thought he was immortal.

SLOWLY ALL THE FAVOR THE ROCK STAR STATUS SLIPPED AWAY AND I BECAME YOUR EVERYDAY GARDEN VARIETY JUNKIE

An earache and a bump on my jaw got me to the doctor one sunny afternoon in paradise. I wasn't ready for the look of concern on the doctor's face. He didn't like what he saw and rushed me in to surgery the next morning. That evening I was told the surgery lasted over eight hours and that they had resuscitated me back to life. Not knowing what was going on, I still felt drugged. My head was wrapped up like a mummy. After ten days the bandages were removed and what I saw was horrifying.

There, staring back at me in the mirror, was a monster. A scar running from the top of my ear down to my Adam's-apple was accented due to the swelling of my face. One eye was stuck, paralyzed wide open, mocking me with fear. My pride melted into horror. This couldn't be me. All those years of being the golden child, the chosen one in the family, destined for greatness, came spiraling down as I imagined my future with a face marred for life. I wanted to die rather than look like this.

Three weeks later my doctor called me in for a meeting. "Scott, you have a rare cancer called Mucadermal Carcinoma. Due to the rapid growth of the tumor in your lymph nodes, you have one to three years maximum to live." He explained that he had removed a large tumor located near my brain. The nerves had been nicked and the right side of my face was paralyzed, and probably wouldn't heal.

Then he added an extraordinary comment, "But I don't believe it has to be this way." All I could hear echoing in my ears was the death sentence, but something inside of me still wanted to live.

Reeling from shock, I recounted the beginning of my drug addiction fifteen years earlier when my mom and grandparents died within a few months of each other. My motto became it is better to go out in a ball of flames rather than rust.

And so I did. What was once a "party addiction" of heroin, cocaine and pills became a way of life, massive amounts. It didn't matter; I was going to die anyway. I pushed away those who loved me. I became so strung-out that I kept a syringe of heroin in the drawer waiting for me so that when I woke up in cold sweats in the middle of the night it would take away the nightmares and send me back into drugged oblivion.

Slowly all the favor, the rock-star status slipped away and I became your everyday garden-variety sleazy junkie. Who could ever love me? I was so addicted there was no way out and I knew I would never be normal again. Demonic activity began to surround me.

Soon I was busted for possession of drugs and so began my life as a prisoner.

It started off as a weekend in jail, and years later I would be bunking in the same prison as Charlie Manson.

During one of my short-term stays in the county jail I found myself drawn to a Bible study with other inmates and learned a little about a Savior I never knew. Later, when I got out on the streets, I tried to keep reading the Bible. I started in the gospels reading Jesus' words in the morning, only to gravitate back to the partying every night. The Bible reading stopped and the partying continued full blast. I quit showing up to my meetings with my probation officer, which put me in violation. I was on the run. My addictions were back full force and I was more desperate than ever. There was nowhere to turn, nowhere to hide.

Having survived an overdose I would later experience a night of terror. In a sober moment, I witnessed with my own eyes occult sacrifices of animals right across the street from my friend's apartment. God taught me an unforgettable lesson in those two events: that Satan was real, and so was hell — and I was going there full speed. He was not willing however that I would perish!

One night I slept under a bush in my hometown, where I had grown up the highly favored great-grandson of one of the most influential men in that city. Look at me now, I thought. I cried and cried. How had it come to this? I had squandered it all — money, looks, influence, education, and the right

God, if you hear me, if you know me, I need you. Please help me. I can't stop these drugs.

upbringing — all of it wasted as I wrestled with my reality under a bush. In that dark, cold night I remembered the God of the red letters in the gospels — the One who had reached out to me in jail, this God who loved me when no one else would. I mustered up my voice and whispered to Him. "God, if you hear me, if you know me, I need you. Please help me. I can't stop these drugs."

A couple days later the police found me. I was busted, with guns drawn, a full fanfare of cops and cars chasing me through a house. This incident brought me to face my greatest fears and yet my greatest desire. I would now experience withdrawal from drugs and my final days living with cancer in a jail cell. My addiction was so severe that I truly believed there was no way I would live through withdrawal, or "the jones" as known to addicts. I knew in three days the withdrawal would be hitting me full force.

There I was, lowering the noose over my head, fitting it around my neck, when the speaker in my solitary glass cell burst with the words "chow call." A buzzer rang and the cell door clicked open. Bewildered and frustrated I took off the noose and ventured out into the main population of convicts. I was drenched in sweat, shaking, having thrown up for three days. Overwhelmed with the fatigue of not sleeping and depression of a dying man, I had no choice but to step in line to the chow hall. It was useless. I could not eat. I could barely sit and focus. My stomach and bowels were exploding and my muscles twitched on the verge of seizure. I would have to wait another hour until the rotation back to the cells. Walking back I was not sure if I had it in me to make another attempt at killing myself.

When the cell door opened, there on my bunk was a Bible. How did it get there? I had no celly (roommate), and the room was completely enclosed in glass. This is what they did with convicts who were considered dangerous to the general population and the state was preparing to ship off to a prison. Yet, there it was: a Bible.

Immediately falling to my knees near the bed I began to weep. This Bible was mine. God was real and He did care about me. I wept and wept, crying out to be forgiven. I wanted to know this loving God who chased me down. Desperately needing Him, He was my only hope to survive. I wept. Hope began to invade my heart. Tears flowed from my eyes as I marveled at how my physical ailments seemed to diminish as I held the Word of God close to my heart.

Looking down at the floor there was a pool of tears on the concrete at least eighteen inches in diameter. Opening the Bible, I began reading from the book of Acts. Here were Christians who had just gone through what appeared to be the most agonizing of circumstances, having watched their Savior crucified.

They felt alone and were not sure what to do next. I related to them. This book continued drawing me in. Reading on I learned about a man named Paul who was imprisoned for loving his Savior. The words were jumping off the pages and ministering to my soul. Each day I physically felt stronger, healthier, and renewed. I was filled with hope and truth. Jesus Christ was my Savior who delighted in leaving the 99 to come find me.

Nothing could stop me from devouring His word. Soon I began to speak with anyone who would listen, inmates and guards. We all needed hope and direction. I spent about a month in county lock-up. This was a time of preparation, equipping me to walk with the God who loved me.

Soon I would be transferring to Chino State Prison, which was a lot scarier than staying in county lock-up. I leaned on God for hope and courage. At Chino they burned my clothing and allowed me one possession, my Bible. I received underwear, pants and a t-shirt. No shoes, jacket or any bedding. The prison reminded me of an old movie with three tiers of cells.

My cell had one bunk, a toilet, a small window in the door and a tiny window on the back wall with the glass broken out. It was barely big enough for one man. On a cold winter night, sitting next to the door as the light spilled onto the pages of my Bible, my God was with me.

Why, Lord, why are you sending me there?

During my twelve-week stay at Chino I had a different roommate every week, all of whom I shared the love of Christ with. At least eight of them began to study the Bible and pray with me each day. Soon I was allowed to go outside and have recreation time. My circle of influence grew and I shared whenever I could. Some looked ready to kill me for doing that, but I was so full of joy being alive I did not care. Surely they needed a Savior too!

Most inmates were classified and shipped off to their permanent housing within ten days of arriving at Chino. I'm not exactly sure why God kept me there that long. There were twelve who were either stoked or suffered being locked up with me. Sharing from the scriptures with greater confidence each day I saw God's favor going before me always.

After twelve weeks I got word that they were transferring me to Corcoran State Prison. When I asked about Corcoran I received many concerned looks, even from the guards. "What's wrong with Corcoran?" I would plead. I came to find out it was the newest prison in the system, designed for hardened criminals with the highest security level, including a death row. Not considered a danger to the system, I was classified as a level one prisoner and should have qualified for a work furlough program. But it never was to happen. Instead I was being shipped to level three at Corcoran with violent criminals. Some notorious figures who lived there were Charlie Manson, Noriega, and Sirhan Sirhan.

I cried out to the Lord. "Why, Lord, why are you sending me there?"

I arrived exhausted after hours of riding on the bus completely shackled down with chains around my waist, hands and feet. Once again, I was stripped of everything I had, except my Bible. I was in solitary lockdown for two weeks with a roommate that looked like Charlie Manson's double. Needless to say there were quite a few restless nights in that cell.

They moved me to new housing and I received freedom to walk the yard. That's when God began to open my understanding of why He brought me to Corcoran. I found out the first day in the yard that there was a chapel. Seeing an open door I yelled, "Praise the Lord!" A convict my age yelled back, "What? Praise the Lord!" His name was Dyon, the chaplain's assistant. He came out with a puzzled look on his face because apparently not many stopped by with that kind of greeting. We soon became fast and best friends. His knowledge of the word was incredible and he began to disciple me. At Corcoran we had the best Christian library in the whole state penal system, and I was accepted into a Bible College program for prisoners.

During August of 1990 I was released from prison with $200 to my name. To be honest I was more anxious about living my Christianity on the streets in the midst of temptation than I was coming into prison on my first day. Thankfully, I had made many friends that were praying for me. The guards took me to the train station and paid for my one-way ticket to Santa Ana. That city happened to be where many of my former drug connections lived. I quickly hopped any bus that would get me away from there.

Finding a motel room for the night, I spent my last fifty bucks. "What should I do, Lord?" I began to pray. Not wanting to contact my old druggie friends, I remembered there was one true friend I could trust. He was responsible, owned a house and his own company. I called him.

He seemed genuinely glad to hear my voice and informed me he had just gotten married. Right now it wouldn't be a good time for me to come by. Completely understanding his position, I explained my new faith in Christ. Thanking him for being a faithful friend through all the years I assured him, "Jesus will take care of me." And then I hung up.

Prayer consumed me all night. Early the next morning as I was leaving the hotel room, I almost shut the door with the key inside when the phone rang. To think I almost missed this call. It was 6:30 in the morning; no one knew I was around. Who could be calling? Grabbing the phone I heard my old friend's voice. "Scott?" he said, "Is that you? I have been up all night calling every hotel in the surrounding cities trying to find you." Apparently I had shared the love of Christ with him but forgot to mention where I was staying.

"After you hung up, my wife and I talked. We decided we want you to move in with us for two months, free room and board. Over that time, if you work for me I'll give you $1000 to go get a place of your own."

All through the years God had provided and cared for my soul! At the end of two months I moved into an apartment in Dana Point where I was to meet my future wife and begin what is now a 20-year ministry with the Lord. God has blessed me with three beautiful children and a chance to know Him, love Him and serve Him. He has never once let me down. Never!

He Calls Us…

Beloved, it is a great and marvelous mystery to be loved by the God of the universe. He calls us His very own: His friends, His kids, co-inheritors of the Kingdom with His Son, Jesus Christ. The King of Kings and Lord of Lords has delighted in walking with me every step of the way. No storm has overtaken me that He has not provided a way through. No trouble has saddened me that He has not caught my every tear and comforted my soul. He has blessed me beyond my wildest dreams. And He wants to bless you!

If you've not met this God of heaven yet, then take a moment to invite Him into your heart. His Son, Jesus, took your every trouble to the cross and willingly paid your price there. He rose on the third day to bring you not only life eternal, but life more abundantly.

I am a living testimony of that grace, a living stone standing here declaring that God is good and He loves you no matter what. He has set this prisoner free. How about you?

A Call To Testify

Annie

Throughout my Christian walk, I have marveled at stories of how God healed someone or brought him or her through a difficult trial. While amazed by these miraculous events, they didn't have quite the same impact until I personally experienced a miracle. I guess it would be similar to comparing an individual who has read or heard about childbirth but never had the experience personally. Until you push that baby out, one can only imagine. My personal journey began in August 2007.

One little staph infection, just the size of a hangnail, blossomed into a year and a half of craziness. We're not talking about mental illness (although at times I may have displayed a lot of unusual behaviors); thankfully my family and friends were kind enough to be somewhat understanding and prayerful.

This was the start of a ten-month round of the little bacteria fighters (antibiotics) with different names and colors for the various maladies that I would experience along the way. In the early stages I attributed my breathing difficulty to the horrible fires in the fall of 2007, but then my symptoms quickly escalated from pneumonia to asthma. To make matters worse, boils began popping up, one by one, covering the back of my head. All along I saw many specialists and took antibiotics daily.

One bright spot, beside these little red volcanoes or boils, was the wonderful surgeon that performed the lancing. I knew she must have a sense of humor as I sat in her consultation room waiting to meet her for the first time. A delightfully placed sign adorned one wall stating boldly: "Hemorrhoids are Fun!" I thought this surgery could be painful, but at least this doctor was amusing.

Being a stranger to poor health, I was hopeful that my prayers would be answered soon and that God would heal me. Over several months I went forward at church to receive prayer and was put on prayer chains as friends were continuously encouraging me to stand firm and be patient.

I GREW closer to HIM during this desert experience

Being sick is not something I was accustomed to, feeling so lousy that you don't want to do anything or go anywhere. My life now was very different. For as long as I could remember I had been blessed with lots of energy, a zest for life and a love of people. The Lord allowed this plague to wean me from my dependence on family, friends and activities as they were held back for a season. I grew closer to Him during this desert experience.

The Lord was strengthening me in the hidden parts of my soul and my character was being fortified. I resolved to make life changes as He was calling me to a deeper place. Many hours, days, then months, were now spent in His presence, meditating on His Word, learning how to pray, and being still before Him. My God was speaking to me and, finally, I was listening.

After months and months of confusing symptoms, they were finally able to discover the root of my illnesses. I was diagnosed with MRSA, a strain of staph bacteria that is resistant to the broad-spectrum antibiotic commonly used to treat it! MRSA can be fatal. No wonder I was sick!

My first personal healing came about midway through a ten-day treatment of drugs. Prescribed by the infectious disease doctor it was a cocktail, a combination of powerful drugs. It felt like drinking the kitchen sink on an empty stomach.

One Sunday a friend invited me to go to Vineyard Community Church. Slipping into my seat, I tried to be as inconspicuous as possible in my tropical headdress, hoping no one would recognize me or ask what was under the scarf.

After a time of singing praises, the pastor addressed the congregation wanting to know if there was anyone who felt discouraged as a result of a long illness. I shot up to my feet, a blasting missile ready to receive that word. Many people circled around me laying their hands on my body as they prayed for Jesus to heal me. They didn't know my condition (except my friend), nonetheless they fervently sought the Lord, praying the blood of Jesus over my body and standing in the authority God has given us to heal the sick.

"And as you preach, 'the kingdom of heaven is at hand.' Heal the sick, cleanse the lepers, raise the dead, cast out demons. Freely you have received, freely give."
Matt 10:7-8 NIV

My faith was built up that day and I left encouraged, but truthfully didn't feel any different physically, that was until the next morning when I woke up. After such a long time I was accustomed to a deep, heavy, anxious feeling that became my norm each day. However, this time something was very different, and as my eyes opened, the rooster crowed like a shofar horn sounding an announcement. I knew without a doubt that something was different. I was healed!

Shortly thereafter, I made an appointment to see my infectious disease doctor who gave me the old swab test in the nose. Apparently this is the best way to determine the MRSA bacteria. The report came back clean, no MRSA, HEALED!

My afterglow resembled a strand of Christmas lights that were burning brightly as I stopped anyone and everyone to tell them: My God Heals! My passion (for the testimony) soared. God allowed this time to weave into my soul the importance of testifying to His miracles, signs and wonders, and how relevant they are for the Church, as well as the up and coming generations. Everything He has imparted to us is NORMAL CHRISTIANITY for today and I wanted to walk in this truth.

Over the next several months, I heard many testimonies. My spiritual senses were being fine tuned as I listened to the hand-printed stories of God. It became everything to me and I couldn't get enough. My biggest cry to God was, "How do we capture them for others to know your glory?"

On May 7, 2009, the Lord downloaded the vision for TESTIFY, the book, to little ol' me. I was overwhelmed upon seeing the activation of His purpose in this vision. He showed me the book, what it looked like in its entirety and how it would contain treasures within. As inadequate as I felt in my own capabilities, how could you say no to the God of the universe after He had miraculously touched so many?

I was overwhelmed and awestruck that He would choose me to be the personal guardian of these treasures as well as the facilitator of this book project. Believe me, I had NO previous experience writing or publishing anything.

During the next few weeks I began to pray with intensity, asking God to give me understanding of this vision. He directed me to people with experience in this field as well as my pastor, who gave me such encouragement and blessings. My heart was full of love for the testimony and somehow He would make it come to pass.

Although my inner man was full of these new promises of God, so full of excitement and purpose, my physical body had been experiencing "revenge of the antibiotics" with stomach issues and constant pain in my arms from all the toxins.

In August, my girlfriends and I decided to attend a women's conference at Bethel Church in Redding, California. We were so excited to be with 1,200 Christian women from all around the world. Personally, I looked forward not only to hearing from the speakers but receiving prayer for healing. My expectancy level was high and faith renewed as I recalled my earlier miracle of healing. Bethel Church had been the site of five hundred healing touches of God during 2008.

"THAT IS SO EASY!"

Sunday, after service, there was a time of prayer in which people were encouraged to come forward. The most unexpected of prayer partners, a young man of size in a bright orange shirt and madras Bermudas, was paired with me. This would be an ordained appointment.

Many people of faith waited patiently in line for their turn to receive prayer. When I arrived at the front I could feel the presence of God. Immersed in the confidence and boldness of the Holy Spirit this young man asked me, "What's up?" I told him of my condition and he looked me straight in the eye, saying, "That is so easy!"

Snapping his fingers, he began praying the promises of God over me. Immediately the power of the Holy Spirit fell. My body quaked and shook from side to side as I experienced a warm sensation coming out of my lower back as the toxins fled.

Walking back to my seat like a drunken sailor, I laid across the chairs for a long time soaking in the presence of the Lord, resting in what just happened. My friend wanted me to talk to her and yet I couldn't. So wrecked was I for a period of time I wasn't sure if I would be able get up and walk to my car let alone drive home. From that time forward I have experienced no pain in my arms and my stomach is healed! Glory to God!

My faith level for God's miracles and the power of the testimony is high. He is so good and faithful to His Word! The Holy Spirit has ignited within me a passion to see other Christians share their precious stories and TESTIFY to God's glory.

"Go home to your family and tell them how much the Lord has done for you and how he has had mercy on you."
Mark 5:19b NIV

Living Stones

Testify

As you come to him, the living Stone—rejected by men but chosen by God and precious to him— you also, like living stones, are being built into a spiritual house to be a holy priesthood ...

1 Peter 2:4-5a NIV

Every day people encounter your life, and like the memorial stones, they see you, a living stone, and ask, "What has happened here?" Let your light shine.

Author's Final Thoughts

Testify

A Testimony is the written or spoken account of anything God has done from the moment you become born again in Christ Jesus. Your hand-printed stories are unique; there is no other one just like yours.

Anyone who believes in the Son of God has this testimony in his heart.
1 John 5:10 NIV

For more information about "Testify the Book", please visit your local bookstore,
testifythebook.com or email us at info@testifythebook.com

God's Promises

To You!

BELIEF

"For God so loved the world that he gave his one and only Son,
that whoever believes in him shall not perish but have eternal life"

.John 3:16 NIV

" 'If you can'?" said Jesus. "Everything is possible for him who believes."

Mark 9:23 NIV

COMFORT

The LORD is good, a refuge in times of trouble.
He cares for those who trust in him,

Nahum 1:7 NIV

"Come to me, all you who are weary and burdened, and I will give you rest."

Matthew 11:28 NIV

COURAGE

He gives strength to the weary and increases the power of the weak.

Isaiah 40:29 NIV

FAITHFULNESS, GOD'S

Let us hold unswervingly to the hope we profess, for he who promised is faithful.

Hebrews 10:23 NIV

Those who know your name will trust in you,
for you, LORD, have never forsaken those who seek you.

Psalm 9:10 NIV

GUIDANCE

Whether you turn to the right or to the left,
your ears will hear a voice behind you, saying, "This is the way; walk in it."

Isaiah 10:21 NIV

Trust in the LORD with all your heart and lean not on your own understanding;
in all your ways acknowledge him, and he will make your paths straight.

Proverbs 3:5-6 NIV

JOY

I have told you this so that my joy may be in you and that your joy may be complete.

John 15:11 NIV

Though you have not seen him, you love him; and even though you do not see him now,
you believe in him and are filled with an inexpressible and glorious joy,

1 Peter 1:8 NIV

LONELINESS

I will not leave you as orphans; I will come to you.

John 14:18 NIV

LOVE, GOD'S

The LORD appeared to us in the past, saying:
"I have loved you with an everlasting love; I have drawn you with loving-kindness.
Jeremiah 31:3 NIV

"The LORD your God is with you, he is mighty to save.
He will take great delight in you, he will quiet you with his love,
he will rejoice over you with singing."
Zephaniah 3:17 NIV

This is love: not that we loved God,
but that he loved us and sent his Son as an atoning sacrifice for our sins.
1 John 4:10 NIV

MERCY

As a father has compassion on his children,
so the LORD has compassion on those who fear him;
Psalm 103:13 NIV

PROTECTION, GOD'S

when you lie down, you will not be afraid; when you lie down, your sleep will be sweet.
Proverbs 3:24 NIV

He will have no fear of bad news; his heart is steadfast, trusting in the LORD.
Psalm 112:7 NIV

SICKNESS

Heal me, O LORD, and I will be healed; save me and I will be saved,
for you are the one I praise.
Jeremiah 17:14 NIV

He himself bore our sins in his body on the tree, so that we might die to sins and live for righteousness;
by his wounds you have been healed.
1 Peter 2:24 NIV